EMMERDALE FARM BOOK 8

THE COUPLE AT DEMDYKE ROW

A Star Original

'I thought it was only right to come and tell you, Mr Gimbel. There's nothing wrong in it ... nothing ...' Joe searched for a word '... nothing dishonourable. As soon as the divorce comes through, Kathy and me'll be wed.'

'No!'

It was a great shout of rejection. It seemed to fill the kitchen, to echo up through the house.

'It's settled, Mr Gimbel. It's no good saying no. We're moving in tomorrow.'

'My daughter going to live with a man outside wedlock –'

'Kathy,' moaned Mrs Gimbel, 'how could you? The disgrace ...'

Also by Lee Mackenzie in *Star*

EMMERDALE FARM No 1: THE LEGACY
EMMERDALE FARM No 2: PRODIGAL'S PROGRESS
EMMERDALE FARM No 3: ALL THAT A MAN HAS ...
EMMERDALE FARM No 4: LOVERS' MEETING
EMMERDALE FARM No 5: A SAD AND HAPPY SUMMER
EMMERDALE FARM No 6: A SENSE OF RESPONSIBILITY
EMMERDALE FARM No 7: NOTHING STAYS THE SAME
ANNIE SUGDEN'S COUNTRY DIARY

EMMERDALE FARM BOOK 8

THE COUPLE AT DEMDYKE ROW

Lee Mackenzie

Based on the successful Yorkshire Television series originated by Kevin Laffan

A STAR BOOK
published by
The Paperback Division of
W.H. ALLEN & Co. Ltd

A Star Book
Published in 1979
by the Paperback Division of
W. H. Allen & Co. Ltd
A Howard and Wyndham Company
44 Hill Street, London W1X 8LB
Reprinted 1979

Made and printed in Great Britain
by The Anchor Press Ltd
Tiptree, Essex

ISBN 0 352 30334 4

CHAPTER ONE

Perhaps it all began because Joe felt they needed a trailer to take livestock to market. To get the cash for the trailer – an expensive thing – it occurred to Joe they might as well sell Hawthorn Cottage. That provided a fund of the kind Emmerdale had never had before. So because he felt as if he had money to spare, Joe got the idea of buying another, smaller place for himself...

It was a bit like that rhyme, 'Because of a nail, the shoe was lost; because of the shoe, the horse was lost...' From small causes, big effects were to come.

But perhaps they'd have come anyhow. Perhaps the moment had arrived when Joe Sugden and Kathy Gimbel were to play out their rôles in the relationship that had been developing for over a year. If it hadn't been a need for money that brought about the sale of Hawthorn, it would have been something else. As Joe looked back on it afterwards, he saw that it was inevitable.

Not that that helped.

The discussion about the trailer began at Sunday lunch one fine summer day. Matt had gone off for one of his long walks – since the tragedy of losing his children he'd taken to spending a lot of time on his own. His place at table was taken by Henry Wilks, who was tucking in with enjoyment.

'I wanted to talk to Matt about the calves,' Henry remarked as he passed his plate for more roast lamb. 'Did I gather from him that you're going to go in for beef rearing?'

'I mind the time when Beckindale beef were famous,' Sam Pearson put in. 'Never much of it, tha knows ... But choice, it were.'

'It's this way,' Joe explained. 'Government's encouraging fat stock at the moment, so I was saying to Matt, I reckon we should go more for beef.'

'If prices I see in shops are owt to go by,' Henry agreed, 'you're right.'

Annie Sugden smiled. 'A farmer never gets as much for meat as the housewife pays for it, Henry. Don't get the idea we'll make a fortune.'

'Nay, I never count my fat stock before it's raised.' He accepted his refilled plate and eyed it with pleasure. 'Can't believe Beckindale beef were a patch on Beckindale lamb. This is great, Annie.'

'Mind you, beef-raising would involve us in some extra expense. We'd not be able to carry on taking stock to market in t'Land-Rover, or wait for the hired truck to arrive. Remember last winter? Got stuck in t'snow down Braik's Bottom.'

'That was a specially bad day. Doesn't often stop transport.'

Sam snorted. 'That's all you know, Henry. Why, I remember when I were a lad, we got snowed up for eight days ...'

'What we need,' Joe said, disregarding his grandfather, 'is a new trailer.'

'Um,' Henry said, concentrating on the mint sauce.

'And they're not cheap.'

'Um.'

'Don't get over-enthusiastic, will you?' Joe said, beginning to laugh.

'Now, Joe, you know I'm always ready to back you up in any good business idea. But at the moment I'm giving my attention to your mother's cooking.'

'What's for afters?' Sam asked.

'Apple pie and Yorkshire cheese.'

'Ah ... In that case I won't have any more lamb.'

In the somnolent atmosphere of good food and summer weather, the discussion about the trailer lapsed. And somehow in the next few days it just wasn't easy to get hold of Henry for a conversation about the funds to buy one – or even whether they were actually going to do so.

'He flits about like a tawny owl.' Joe complained to Matt as they mucked out the mistle a few days later. 'Tells you he's behind you if it's good business, then you can never get hold of him to find out whether he thinks it *is*.'

'Ah, you know Henry,' Matt said. Matt seldom had a hard word to say about anything. Even the death of his little Sally and Sam had not embittered him. He was quieter these days – but then he'd never been talkative,

'What d'you think, Matt?'

'About what? Raising beef, or trailer?'

'Beef.'

'Well, we've had good results with those three calves we kept. Seems to me it's no harder to raise a bull calf than a milker. Prices are rising. So ... aye, I'm in favour of going in for fat stock.'

'It follows from that that we have to have transport. Doesn't it?'

'Ye-es.'

'So what we need is a new trailer.'

'I suppose so. It'll cost a thousand pounds or more, though.'

Joe sighed. 'Yeah ...'

'Put it to Henry, then.'

'Makes me a bit fed up, always having to go to Henry for any sum higher than fifty quid.'

Matt went to the tap and turned on the water for the hose. 'He don't mind. He feels that's his part in running things.'

Joe studied Matt's round, quiet face. 'Never makes you feel we're ... sort of taking a soft option?'

'How d'you mean?'

'Other farmers have to run things so they can finance their own improvements. We just turn to Henry.'

'He is part of the farm, Joe.'

'I'm not saying he isn't. I'm just saying that we rely on him too much where money's concerned. We ought to look at our assets in a proper light, not just turn to Henry with a hand out.'

Matt looked a little surprised. 'Have you said all this to Ma?

She thinks a lot of Henry's judgement.'

'So do I,' Joe said quickly. 'Don't get me wrong, Matt. But I've been having a think, and it seems to me we could finance this new trailer another way. But it's something I need to ask Ma about. I'll have a word with her this morning.'

But this wasn't to be. As she was serving breakfast, Annie had a phone call from their neighbour, Freda Gimbel. 'I'm just a bit under the weather again,' Freda said, in the faint, helpless voice she'd learned to assume when she wanted something. 'It'd be a kindness if you'd drop in, Annie. Only if you've the time, of course. I don't want to be a burden.'

'It's no trouble, Freda,' Annie said, although it was – she'd intended to get the curtains down and through the washing machine today, since the sun was so bright and a good breeze was blowing.

When the men had been fed and her father was settled in his toolshed sharpening the shears for a go at the thorn hedge, Annie took off her apron and headed for the Gimbels' farm by way of the footpath past the oak tree. She paused under its boughs to gaze up at the sky. There was something wonderful to her in the rustling of the leaves, the cool greenness against the blue of the summer sky. 'God's in his heaven, All's right with the world,' she quoted to herself as she walked on.

But all was not right in the Gimbels' world. Freda Gimbel had had a genuine heart murmur during the winter, which had meant a stay in hospital and some gentle advice from the specialist to take things easier. It's seldom possible to take things easy on a farm, but the Gimbel family had done their best to lighten the burden. Yet in a house with so few modern improvements, housework was hard work; Annie looked about with secret dismay at the old-fashioned sink in the kitchen, the old-fashioned wash-boiler glimpsed through the scullery door . . .

In a way she didn't blame Freda for playing up her ill-health. She couldn't help thinking that if she had to get up day after day to wrestle with that old-fashioned coal range, she might decide to be 'poorly' quite often.

She could never make up her mind whether Freda was acting or not. Today she certainly looked peaky. 'It's just that I . . . I never seem to have a moment to recover myself,' she complained. 'It's one thing after another . . . And with no woman in the house to help me . . . It's hard, Annie.'

Annie was in the same situation – no woman to help her. She had the same number of men to look after – her father, Joe, and Matt. Freda had her husband Jim and two sons, Martin and Davey. Yet Annie felt she was in a much better position than Freda. There was a cheerfulness at Emmerdale which compared favourably with the grudging, dreary atmosphere at Holly Farm. And now that Joe was making the farm pay, he never withheld any improvement she asked for. Annie now had a freezer to ease her catering problems, and a washing machine to cope with the unending stream of dirty clothes, and a dryer for the wet days of winter . . .

Poor Freda. Annie reproached herself for being sceptical about her ill-health. All the same, she stopped herself from offering actual physical help with the housework. She really did have enough of her own. 'Couldn't you get Jim to let you have a woman come in a couple of times a week?' she inquired.

'Who'd come?' Freda rejoined.

Who, indeed? To this cheerless house? Annie sighed. Domestic help was scarce and expensive, in any case.

'What I was thinking,' Freda said, patting nervously at her hair, 'was that if we could get Kathy to come home . . .'

Her daughter had left during the winter, driven away by the continual disapproval from Jim Gimbel because of her 'past'. Kathy, like many a girl, had married the wrong man – a shotgun wedding brought about at her father's insistence. She'd had a miscarriage, the marriage showed itself to be a total mistake, and Terry had simply walked out. It wasn't to be wondered at that Kathy found she had a lot in common with Joe Sugden, who also had a broken marriage behind him. The village of Beckindale had watched expectantly as these two drifted together, and didn't know whether to be disappointed or approving when Kathy removed herself to a job in Hotten.

Annie looked at Kathy's mother. 'I don't really think Kathy would want to come back,' she said in a tone of gentle reproof, 'not after the way she was treated.'

'Well, you see ... I had a word with Jim ... I said to him, I said, "Look, Jim, you've got to see it my way," I said, "I can't go on like this ..." And after all, Annie, blood is thicker than water.'

But much messier, thought Annie. 'Have you written to her?' she inquired.

'Nay, letter writing's no good. And she's not on t'phone, except in that coffee-bar – and you can't speak to her about a private matter on a phone in a coffee-bar.'

'I suppose not.'

'What I was thinking,' said Freda, looking even more nervous, 'was that if *you* had a word with her –'

'Me?' Annie was astounded.

'Well, after all, you *are* church-warden, and in any case, she'd listen to you – she's always thought a lot of you, Annie. More than she has of me.' Freda's hand stroked and patted her greying hair. 'We're not close, me and Kathy. I dunno why ... But she's a good girl, really, no matter what Jim feels about the mistakes she's made. And if you put it to her that I need her, she'll come back.'

'But I don't know if it would be right to bring her back,' Annie said, quite blunt.

Freda coloured. And at that moment Annie wondered if perhaps she really was less well than the last time she'd seen her. There was a tense, nervy look about her as she flushed. It couldn't be good for a woman with a heart condition to be getting herself in a state ...

'Jim's promised not to be hard on her,' she said. 'She won't have to put up with criticism.'

'I wonder if Jim would be able to keep quiet when he sees something he thinks is sinful?' Annie remarked. 'He's always been one to speak his mind. And unfortunately he thinks so many ordinary things are sinful, Freda – transistor radios, television, staying out after ten at night, women drinking in a pub ... When I said I wondered if it would be right to bring Kathy back, I was thinking about what she'd be giving up, really. In Hotten she can please herself what she does with her spare time. Here, she'd have to stay within her father's rules – if she had any spare time, that is.'

'I've told you, Jim's said he'll be reasonable about all that. He understands he's a bit behind the times on some things ... Please talk to her, Annie. If you don't, I can't think what I'll do!'

There was just enough veiled threat in this to worry Annie. Was Freda suggesting she might take too many of the pills given her by her doctor? Or just that she'd walk out? Or what?

It was too much of a risk to take. Annie discussed the matter for a few minutes longer but agreed to go to Hotten to speak to Kathy. 'But I must get home now, Freda. I've got a casserole in the oven.'

'You're a good friend, Annie.' Freda pressed her hand as she saw her out.

The last impression Annie had was of a pile of ironing on the lid of the wash-copper, waiting to be done. Perhaps Freda really wasn't fit enough to be standing at an ironing board for an hour or more ... Perhaps; but then again, perhaps she was just feeling lonely and put-upon.

After the midday meal Annie drove to Hotten. By the time she got there the lunch-time crowd had left the coffee-bar and it was almost deserted, although there were dozens of used cups on the tables waiting to be cleared. Kathy was piling them on a tray as Annie came in.

'Hello, Mrs Sugden!' she said with obvious pleasure, shaking back her soft straight hair. She hadn't a free hand to put it out of her eyes. Annie did it for her, making the act almost like a motherly caress. Kathy smiled at her. 'Come in for a coffee? Have one on the house!'

'Thanks, love, I'd like that. Any chance of a word?'

'Oh, well ... I ...' Kathy held up the laden tray. 'I'm paid to clear up this lot.'

'I came on purpose when I thought you wouldn't have many customers.'

'Oh, I see.' Kathy understood this wasn't just a casual visit. 'Tell you what, sit down a minute and I'll ask Mrs Small.'

The manageress was struggling with refills for the coffee urn. 'I really need that washing-up done, Kathy.'

'All right if I take Mrs Sugden into the kitchen to talk while I do it?'

'No customers in the back premises ... Oh, all right, but don't make a habit of it.'

Annie was quite intrigued to be taken into the clinical-looking kitchen. She remembered these premises when they used to be an old-fashioned haberdasher's. Now it was all white melamine and chrome, with an electric water-heater that hissed steamy water to wash and sterilise the cups and saucers. Kathy put the crockery in the big sink, ran in the boiling water, then – to Annie's amusement – made coffee for them with a kettle and instant powder.

'Sugar? No, you don't ... I'm giving it up too,' Kathy said. Kathy was always going on a diet, although Annie could never see the need, for the girl was as slim as a colt.

'I was talking to your mother this morning,' Annie began. 'She's not too well, Kathy.'

Kathy sighed and put her cup down with a bang. 'I might have known it,' she exclaimed. 'She sent you, didn't she?'

'Yes, but –'

'I'm not going back. I'm not living through all that again, Mrs Sugden.'

'I understand how you feel, Kathy. I told your mother I wasn't sure it would be right to bring you back to that situation. But she seemed so ...'

'She puts it on,' Kathy said in a hard voice. 'You don't know her. Ever since she had that heart trouble, she's seen it as a great method of getting her own way.'

'Now, Kathy,' Annie said with some reproach. 'You can't say she gets her own way! If she did, that place would be a lot more comfortable. She's really got a hard life there, love.'

'Well, she gets her own way as far as it's possible for anyone to do it, against Dad. She makes him feel guilty for not being able to afford modern equipment – and now she's talked him into agreeing that I can come home. That's it, isn't it?'

'I don't know the ins and outs of it. All I know is that when I saw her this morning she asked me to talk to you about it. And I'm doing that.'

'I won't go back,' Kathy said.

'That's up to you, of course.'

'Is she ill? Or just putting it on?'

'How do I know, Kathy? I'm no doctor.'

'But what did you think?' Kathy hesitated then said, 'Of course you wouldn't want to say if you thought she was shamming.'

'For what it's worth ... I thought she'd gone downhill a bit since last time I talked to her. I saw her in church two Sundays ago and she didn't look bad, then she missed last Sunday – perhaps she didn't feel up to it. But this morning I really thought ... well, I thought she seemed a bit down.'

'It's just that Dad's been getting at her for something, I bet. She's down in the dumps.'

'Even if it's that – it's not good for her, Kathy. You know, she does have something wrong with her. She wasn't in hospital last winter for nothing.'

'I know that, but – Oh, hell!' The word, so unexpected from Kathy, startled Annie. The girl flashed her a look of apology. 'I'm sorry. I feel I'm being blackmailed.'

'I understand how you feel.'

'Another thing, Mrs Sugden ... Me and Joe ...'

'What about you and Joe?'

'Well, if we're thrown together again ...'

'But you've been seeing him, haven't you? He's mentioned you – he's been to Hotten to take you out quite a lot. It's not as if you've been at the other end of the world, Kathy.'

Kathy Gimbel sat with her head bent, not wanting to meet Annie's eye. She wondered if Annie understood the strength of the attraction between her son and Kathy. There had been a suggestion that Joe's wife, Christine, might name Kathy in the divorce suit – and if she had done so, she'd have been justified, in a way. Although Joe's marriage had foundered before ever Kathy and Joe became fond of each other, as Christine herself must have known.

A multiplicity of reasons had forced Kathy to the decision to leave Beckindale. Not least of them was to find out how much she cared for Joe, and how much Joe cared for her. Kathy hadn't wanted to be involved again, not just yet. Her marriage to Terry had scarred her, had left her uncertain of her ability to judge and evaluate. Emotion was too difficult to control in the wake of a broken marriage. So she'd been quite glad to escape to Hotten, and see Joe only intermittently.

During the past months, her feeling for Joe Sugden had become quite recognisable to herself. When she saw him, her heart lifted. When he rang her, his voice made her go weak at the knees. Sometimes she dreamed about him.

She was in love with Joe. She felt almost sure Joe was in love with her. And when they were both free again, she expected Joe to propose.

Now, allowing for the complication of the delay due to the divorce proceedings, all this was quite straightforward. All she had to do was wait until the decree was granted, and they could be married. In a way, she and Joe had gone through a formal courtship since she moved to Hotten.

What would happen if they were living in Beckindale, on adjoining farms, she didn't quite know. She had a feeling it would all become unmanageable.

Yet she was attracted by the idea. To have Joe within daily contact; to be able to happen on him while walking to the village, or in the Woolpack; to be able to spend five minutes talking to him instead of having to make cumbrous arrangements to meet; all this was tempting, even though to get it she would have to go back to the dreary household at Holly Farm.

'What does Joe say?' she asked Annie.

'I haven't spoken to him about it.'

'Happen he'd rather I stayed away – at least until after the divorce.'

Annie laughed. 'You know better than that, Kathy.' Then, seriously: 'It's nowt to do with Joe at this point, my dear. It's a matter of duty. It's whether you see it as your duty to come home, or not.'

'What do you think on't?'

'Nay, I'm not going to say what I think. This is for you to decide.'

'You think I ought to come, don't you?'

'I'm not giving an opinion on that. But I will just say this, Kathy. If your mother were to be rushed to hospital again, would you be easy in your conscience?'

Kathy put her hands up to her face. 'It's not fair!' she cried. 'I've a life of my own to live!'

'There's few of us can live our lives without reference to other folks, I'm afraid.'

She said no more while Kathy sat in thought, her hands clasped close to her mouth almost as if she were praying for guidance. At last, with a very deep sigh, the girl got to her feet. 'I'll go and speak to Mrs Small,' she said. 'I doubt she'll be very pleased about this. Can you take me back now?'

'If you like. What about your things?'

'Oh, I'll just pack a few. I'm not coming back to stay for ever, you know!'

But when she walked into the kitchen at Holly Farm and saw how much needed doing, she had the awful feeling that her stay would be longer than a few days. Her mother actually hugged her, an action so unusual that she knew things had been going badly.

'You're a mug,' her brother Martin said to her when she went out to find him in the barn. 'You'll get the hard end of everything, as usual. Why didn't you stay in Hotten?'

'I dunno, Martin. I just had the feeling that Annie Sugden thought I ought to come back.'

'Well, I don't know how Dad will take it, but Davey'll be

pleased. He's been condemned to do the vegetables every day, and he hates it.'

'Meaning I'll have to take it on now, I suppose.'

'Well, at least you'll leave more on the potatoes when you peel them.' Martin paused to wipe sweat from his forehead. 'I'm glad you're back, Kath. At least you don't grumble all the time.' After turning to pick up his fork, he paused again. 'Seen Joe?'

'Not yet.'

'I think he's over at Hawthorn. Some feller was asking the way there just after dinner-time – Stubbs, I think his name is. I got the impression he wanted to buy it.'

'Buy Hawthorn?' she gasped. 'They're selling it?'

'Dunno. It's the other way round, happen – someone wants to make an offer.'

Kathy shook her head. She'd recovered from the surprise. 'They won't sell Hawthorn,' she said.

She was wrong there. Because Joe needed money to finance the buying of the new trailer, he was listening with some interest to Tom Stubbs as he set forth the idea of selling the cottage.

It was a place where much had happened that was important to the members of the Emmerdale household. Matt Skilbeck had lived there briefly with his wife Peggy before a brain haemorrhage carried her off. Joe had lived there with Christine during their short marriage. Joe had lived on there alone ever since, and Kathy had spent many happy times with him within its strong grey walls.

But the moment comes when a house no longer welcomes its owner. To Joe, Hawthorn was no longer home. He spent more time at Emmerdale than he did at the cottage.

So this was how it came about that he said at tea that evening: 'I think I'll move my gear gack to the attic bedroom, Ma. It makes more sense to be on the spot – if that's all right with you.'

Annie, putting cold ham out on plates, paused in her work. 'You know you're always welcome in your own home, Joe.'

'About time,' grumbled her father. 'Trotting back and forth to Hawthorn ... Doesn't make sense ... You never should have settled there in t'first place.'

'Now, Dad!'

'Well, a farmer should be on his land, not t'other side of four fields!'

'I was wondering ...' Joe stopped what he was saying, and glanced at Matt with a troubled face.

'Wondering what?' Matt inquired.

'I was wondering whether ... you'd mind, Matt, if we sold Hawthorn.'

An extraordinary stillness fell on those around the table. Matt had had so much unhappiness in his life; was it fair to ask him to think back on it, reminding him of the short time he and Peggy had lived there?

Matt picked up his knife and set it down carefully in its place. His fair hair caught a ray of evening sunshine.

'It's nowt to do with me, personally,' he said at last. 'T'cottage belongs to Emmerdale Farm Limited.'

'Nay, it's not just a business decision. I'd want to know if you'd feel ... well, hurt ...'

Matt smiled. 'Don't be daft. Any case, it's more your home than it ever was mine.'

'Then you would go along with the idea of selling?'

'What brought this on?'

'That feller that's coming in as manager at Verney's – Tom Stubbs. He was saying this afternoon he's seen the cottage as he drives past and wondered whether it was being used. Just shows you,' Joe added, without bitterness, 'how much it looks like a home! I'm never there, really. Well, anyway, it struck me ... If we sold Hawthorn, we'd get the money to buy the new trailer, and more besides.'

'Oh, more,' Annie put in, regaining her voice now that the novelty had worn off. 'These days, a place like Hawthorn would fetch a good price.'

'Rubbish. Who'd want a place like that, miles away from t'village?'

'Lots of folk, Grandad. "Away from it all" – that's what they're after these days.'

'More money than sense, then. I think you'll find nobody wants it.'

'Tom Stubbs wants it.'

'Huh. He hasn't seen inside, though.'

'It's not as bad as that, Grandad,' Joe protested. 'I may be living a bachelor existence, but Ma keeps the place tidy.'

'Do you really think it would fetch much?' Matt said.

'Three or four thousand, happen.'

'Delusions of thingummy,' snorted Sam. 'Three or four thousand? They'd want their heads looking, anybody that'd pay that.'

'I think he's right, Dad,' Annie remarked.

'One thing, though,' Matt said.

'What?'

'Happen Henry wouldn't go along with it.'

Joe looked stubborn. 'It's not just what Henry thinks,' he said. 'I got a more or less definite expression of interest from Tom Stubbs this afternoon. I'm showing him round tomorrow.'

'Then what happens if Henry says we're not to sell?'

'We'll put it to a vote.'

'Really got the bit between your teeth, haven't you?' Sam said. He chewed his ham thoughtfully. 'Three or four thousand, eh? You know I remember when Jamieson bought it, in the twenties. Hundred and eight pounds, I think he paid.'

'But it had no water laid on then, Grandad – no electric or anything. 'Sides, even for a downright hovel, they're paying fancy prices these days.'

Annie was covertly watching Matt, who had still not made much headway with his food. She worried about him these days. He was thinner, and he worked too hard.

He glanced up and caught her eye. 'It might be nice to see a proper family living there,' he murmured. 'It *ought* to be a happy place.'

She relaxed. He really wouldn't mind if the house were to change hands. She said to Joe, 'But you've got to speak to Henry before you go too far with this.'

'Oh . . . humph . . . yes . . . well . . .' Joe applied himself to his tea. His grandfather supplied a diversion by telling him how to organise the removal of his belongings from Hawthorn to the attic bedroom.

It wasn't until Joe was going out to make his way to Hawthorn that Annie remembered she had news for him. She hurried after him, catching him up as he was about to get into his car.

'Joe!'

'What? You want me to do something?'

'Joe – I meant to tell you. I was in Hotten this afternoon.'

'Oh yes?'

'Freda Gimbel asked me to talk to Kathy.'

'Oh.' This was a much more guarded note. He frowned, waiting for the rest.

'Kathy's come home, Joe.'

'Home?'

'To Holly Farm.'

The frown vanished. A dawning smile came in its place. 'Well, I'll go to foreign parts! She's back?'

'Listen, Joe, you know how touchy Jim Gimbel can be. Think on.'

'Aye.' He looked serious again. 'Poor lass. Life's never easy for her, is it, Ma.'

She might have replied that it wasn't easy for most folk. But she laid a hand on his sleeve. 'I wanted to tell you when there was no one by. Her mother's poorly, Joe. She'll have her hands full.'

'I know what you mean.' He nodded in understanding then smiled. 'All the same, I'm glad she's back.'

As she went indoors again to side the dishes, his mother couldn't help feeling a bit apprehensive. As if it wasn't enough that Kathy was back to complicate Joe's life, he'd got this notion to hurry ahead with selling the cottage, almost without regard to Henry Wilks.

One thing you could say for Joe. Once he'd got the bit between his teeth, there was no holding him.

CHAPTER TWO

Anxious that Henry's feelings shouldn't be hurt, Annie sought an opportunity to tell him of Joe's plans about the cottage. But the opportunity didn't arise until the evening of the following day, when she went along to the Woolpack to see him.

As soon as she came in, he invited her into the back parlour. He was unsmiling. She took off her coat and sat down, watching him. 'I've got something to tell you about an idea of Joe's,' she began.

'About Hawthorn Cottage?' he broke in.

'You know? He said at tea he hadn't spoken to you yet.'

'Nor has he. I heard it from Lucy Stubbs.'

'Lucy Stubbs? She's some relation of the Tom Stubbs . . . ?'

'His sister. She's with the Advisory and Development Service – stopped in here for a drink at lunchtime today and told me her brother was up there at Hawthorn looking over with a view to buying it.' Henry drew in a breath, puffed out his cheeks, and let it go again. 'I can tell you, Annie, it was a bit of a facer.'

'He intended to talk to you, Henry. He told us he –'

'Told you? Who, exactly?'

'Me and Matt – and Dad.'

'I see. So everybody gets to hear of it except me.'

'It's not that he doesn't want to consult you –'

'*Consult* me? That's what you do when you want an opinion. I've got a *vote*, Annie.'

'Of course he knows that, Henry. He only thought –'

'He cares so little about it that he goes ahead and fixes a buyer.'

'Nay, he's only shown Mr Stubbs round the place. Nothing's fixed.'

'The principle's the same. What happens if after all this I say I'm against selling it?'

'It would have to go to a meeting, formally.'

'Aye, and have a vote.' Henry paused in his indignation to take a look at Annie. 'How would you vote?'

'To tell the truth, I'd be glad to see it go. It's not been a happy place for t'family. Matt and Peg, Joe and Christine –'

'Joe and Kathy,' he put in.

She drew her brows together. 'That's different,' she said. 'That's not our business.'

'I'm sorry. I shouldn't have mentioned that.' Truth was, he was angry – hurt and angry. This was what came of mixing business and sentiment. He'd let himself get too fond of the folk at Emmerdale. It hadn't occurred to him that Joe would forge ahead with any plan without asking his permission. 'Well, so if Joe has got a buyer, we're going to part with Hawthorn, are we?'

But matters fell out in a slightly different fashion. Tom Stubbs loved the cottage, but it simply wasn't big enough for his family. 'I've a wife and a mother-in-law and three kids,' he explained with a rueful laugh. 'We need more bedrooms than you've got.'

'You could build on,' Joe suggested, sorry to let the sale escape him now that he'd made up his mind to it.

'But you need permission for that and it takes ages. Nay, Sugden – I'm sorry, because it's a grand place and my kids would thrive in a spot like this. But I reckon I'll have to stay on in a wing of the Hall until I find something bigger.'

The Hall, the manorial residence of the Verney family, had been sold at last. It was to be remodelled as a college, and Stubbs was to supervise the alterations. His sister Lucy was staying with him at the Hall – a fact which, surprisingly, seemed to please Matt Skilbeck.

'She's training, you see,' he explained to Joe, who listened with a suppressed smile. 'This is her area. So she's putting up with her brother in the meantime.'

'She anything like her brother?' Joe inquired. thinking of the big, burly man.

'Nay, she's little – quite a titch. Knows a lot about farming, though. I had a long conflab with her last night in the Woolpack.'

It was the first time in months Matt had shown an interest in anything or anyone outside Emmerdale. Joe felt a little surge of happy relief. His brother-in-law was going to recover from the deeply-hidden grief of the twins' death.

Annie came in search of Joe, to report to him that Henry knew about the proposed sale of the cottage. 'I felt I ought to tell him before anybody else did,' she explained. 'But I was too late. Lucy Stubbs had already mentioned it.'

'Oh, heck,' groaned Joe.

'You ought to have brought Henry in from the outset, Joe.'

'I'd be glad to,' he burst out. 'But he's never *there*, is he?'

'He was there last night, when I went to look for him.'

'Aye, but when I went the night before, he was out having dinner with friends in Connelton. And during that day he was in Bradford. And when I wanted to talk to him about t'trailer, he was busy over something to do with t'shop.'

Annie sighed. 'That all sounds as if you were trying to talk yourself into being right,' she said. 'The fact is, Henry's put out. You'd best get there and have a conversation.'

Joe rang the Woolpack. Rather to his surprise, Henry himself answered. 'I'd like a word with you, Henry –'

'And I'd like a word with you, young man.'

'When?' Joe said, very terse.

'Right away.'

Annoyed at being treated like a naughty schoolboy, Joe rejoined, 'You'll be there when I get there, will you?'

'You can take a bet on it,' Henry said grimly.

They weren't in the best of moods when they sat down face to face in the back parlour. Henry had cleared the little table which served himself and Amos Brearley as writing desk and dining-table, and had put out a pad and two pencils. It looked rather forbidding.

'Now then,' he began without preamble, 'about this sale of Hawthorn –'

'It isn't sold.'

'No? Your mother told me –'

'Tom Stubbs turned it down. Not big enough.'

'Ah. Do I take it you're dropping the idea?'

'Not a bit –'

'Well, in that case, I'll go on with what I was about to say. A major decision must be taken by the board of the company, and this is a major decision.'

'I'm aware of that. I hadn't got far enough with it to bring it to the board.'

'As I understand it, you've discussed it with everyone.'

'Well . . . I've mentioned it.'

'But not to me.'

'No. But you know I would have.'

'When you got round to it.'

'You've got it all wrong. I want to discuss things with you but I can never get hold of you.'

'I'm always to be reached here, Joe. If I'm not in, you could always leave a message.'

'Oh aye,' Joe said, beginning to feel hot under the collar. 'And what way is that to run a farm? What would happen if something went wrong with one of the milking machines and I said to Matt "Leave a message"?'

'That's not the point. I'm not involved in day-to-day contact with machinery. But I am involved in the disposal of large sums of money, and I want to be kept informed.'

'You're informed now –'

'Joe!' Henry didn't raise his voice, but there was something in his manner that silenced his hearer. 'You don't know too much about boardroom etiquette, so let me tell you a couple of things. It's considered unfair tactics to get everyone else on to your side before telling the other member of the board. If you do that, it means I've got to get the others to change their minds if I don't agree. If you want to put something to the board, it has to be fair do's.'

Joe coloured a little, but refused to back down. 'You've heard about it now. And no sale has been arranged – you can stop it if you want to.'

'I don't want to. You can sell Hawthorn and get the money for your cattle trailer and the other things you want. But only if the right price is right for the cottage. Understand?'

'I'd have come to you on the price,' Joe said, trying to make things clear. 'You know I would.'

'Do I know that? You've taken me by surprise over this, if you want to hear the truth.'

'I . . . I didn't see it that way. It was just that I didn't want to have to come to you for money again.'

'You decided instead to sell part of the assets! *Our* assets, Joe – mine as well as yours.'

'But only for re-investment, Henry –'

'Depends how much you get, whether the re-investment pays off.'

'I'd have cleared that with you. I don't see what all the fuss is about –'

'Then I'll give you a little lesson in business, Joe,' Henry said, still very tart in his manner. 'Hawthorn is a very good property. It will probably fetch a good price and, if kept, would only increase in value. Your cattle trailer will be useless in ten years. The rest of the money, if you use it, becomes risk capital – it stands or falls by the profit you make with it – or the loss. And when I say "you", I mean "us", because we're a company, Joe. What you do with the money you get for Hawthorn involves all of us. And I don't like it when the first I hear of your plans is over a drink with a stranger in the public bar.'

Joe sat staring at him, appalled. The ramifications were startling. But more astounding was Henry's manner. In all the time he'd known him, he'd never heard so much steel in his voice.

Henry, having put him where he belonged, relented. He allowed himself a faint smile. 'Don't look so set down, lad,' he said. 'In business – and you've just taken a big step into "business" – you can't afford a thin skin.'

Joe rallied. 'You don't think you're showing one?' he inquired.

'Me?'

'Getting so much up in the boughs because I took some steps without first telling you?'

'I'm taking my stand – just as you've taken yours,' Henry said. 'You say you don't want to keep coming to me for money – very well. I'm prepared to stand back and let you find money as you think fit. But remember that it was you who took this first step.'

'I'm not apologising for wanting to stand on my own feet.'

'And I'm not apologising for letting you have my opinion.'

'Does that make us even?' Joe asked, with a faint grin.

'Happen it does.' Henry held out his hand. 'But be warned – if you can't take it, don't hand it out.'

Bemused, Joe accepted and shook hands. 'You've made me feel a right beginner.'

'You're not doing so badly! Many another man would have crumbled when I fixed him with my beady eye.'

Joe didn't confess that considerable crumbling *had* gone on inside him. They settled down to discuss the best way of disposing of Hawthorn, and ended with the agreement that Joe should go to an estate agent in Hotten, to place the property in his hands.

He returned home for tea looking stunned. 'D'you know what he told me?' he reported. 'Hawthorn Cottage should go for not less than fourteen thousand quid.'

His grandfather, having just swallowed a mouthful of tea, promptly choked.

'Hey-up, Grandad,' Matt said, thumping him on the back. 'Don't end your days before we've got the money to throw about.'

'Fourteen thousand?' repeated Annie, incredulous.

'Probably more. I couldn't believe it.'

'He's having you on,' Sam said, having recovered the power of speech.

'Nay, he meant it. He got all worked up about the property. Ideal site, nice bit of land around it, garden with flowers and shrubs –'

'*I* planted them,' Sam reminded him.

'Yeah, you did, Grandad, and you've put another thousand on the price, by what I can gather. I can tell you, I couldn't believe it. Even the fact that the place is near two hundred years old puts the price up.'

'Well, I'll believe it when I see it,' his grandfather rejoined.

After tea Joe was due to go for some cricket practice, since the great match for the Butterworth Ball was soon to take place. Same Pearson was the organiser – or at least, he took it upon himself to order everybody about. While Joe waited for his turn at the nets, he went for a stroll. That was how he at last came face to face with Kathy Gimbel.

She was sitting on the grass by the pitch roller, hands clasped round her knees, studying a butterfly on a grass-stem. The butterfly flew off as Joe approached. Kathy looked up.

'Hello, Joe.'

'Hello, Kath.' He slumped down beside her on the grass. 'Didn't know you were interested in cricket.'

She laughed, with some bitterness. 'Oh, fascinated. It just made a good excuse to get out of the house, that's all.'

'Oh?' he said, with immediate sympathy in the dark eyes. 'Things bad at home, are they?'

'You know what it's like.' She shrugged. 'I think it's even worse than when I went away.'

'I was surprised when I heard, Kathy.'

'Yes, I was a bit surprised myself. I meant never to come back, you know.'

'Beckindale isn't all bad, though. There are some good places.'

'Name one!'

'Wherever you are, is a good place, Kathy. It's nice having you around.'

She sighed, and allowed herself to lean against him. He put an arm around her. 'That's better,' he said. 'You're not so angry now.'

'It's not anger, Joe. It's ... oh, I don't know ... utter misery. And there's no place to go to get away from it.'

He hugged her a little. 'There's Hawthorn.'

She looked up at him. 'I hear you're selling up?'

He nodded. 'It seemed a good idea. Nothing ever seemed to go right there – 'cept you and me.'

'We had some happy times, didn't we?'

'Aye ...' They were silent. 'Come for a drink after the practice?'

'What, and start the gossips off again? I left Beckindale to get away from all that.'

'What do they matter?' he challenged.

'They do matter, Joe. While I'm staying with my Dad, it it matters what people say about me.'

'All right then, we'll go somewhere out of t'village. I'll pick you up after the game, and we'll go somewhere else – Connelton or summat.'

'I don't know ...'

'Come on, Kathy. You need something to take you out of yourself.'

'Yes, all right,' she said, suddenly taking the plunge. 'I'll meet you by the bridge.'

'That's the girl!' He scrambled up, seeing his grandfather in the distance gazing about for his team members. He stooped to kiss her briefly before running to join the team.

His grandfather, watching him, was shaking his head. He'd seen the kiss; it was all *wrong*. These two were married folk – and not married to each other!

The next few weeks went by without much drama, if you discounted the match for the Butterworth Ball. The main event otherwise was the death of Percy Edgar, a highly-respected citizen of Beckindale who had been the 'stringer' for the *Hotten Courier*. Amos Brearley only learned of this aspect of Mr Edgar's character when a full-time reporter from Hotten came into the Woolpack, to hear the details of the cricket match.

'Used to get all this from old Percy,' he said over a complimentary pint. 'Comes better from a chap that knows the village, y'see. We'll miss him, old Percy.'

'You'll have to find someone else,' Amos said, quite intrigued at this insight into the workings of the press.

'Where? Tell me that? It has to be someone who knows all that's going on in the district. Now Percy was ideal. Being retired, you see, he used to trot round to all the local shindigs and exhibitions and what-not. Not many folk have the time for it. It's either got to be a retired chap or someone who gets to hear all the local news.'

'Eh?' said Amos, a great light dawning.

'Well, thanks for the beer,' the reporter said, pushing himself erect from the bar. 'If you hear of anybody that would like to give it a try, put him in touch. *Hotten Courier*, High Street, Hotten.'

'I will,' said Amos, 'I will. What would he ... er ... have to do?'

'Oh, just find out what's been happening. Write up a nice little piece. Names and details of prizes won – that kind of thing. Nothing to it, really. Well, so long.'

'So long.'

Amos was entranced. Who had better opportunities than the proprietor of a public house to learn what was going on in the village? A great new future opened out before him. He could see his name in print already: From Our Own Correspondent, Amos Brearley.

Another point of interest, although not to Amos, was the fact that Percy Edgar had had a cottage in Demdyke Row, Beckindale. The cottage was now up for sale.

Kathy and Joe had come even closer since her return to Holly Farm. After their first evening together, it seemed only right that they should spend every moment together that they could contrive. By and by the moment came when, at the end of the evening, they didn't want to part. Hawthorn was still unsold – standing empty and cheerless, but a place where they could be with each other.

Getting up next morning to get ready for milking, Matt looked in at the attic room, intending to rouse Joe. His bed hadn't been slept in. Matt drew back, frowning a little, even shocked. Somehow it hadn't seemed to matter what Joe did while he was living at Hawthorn, but now he'd moved back into Emmerdale it seemed only right that he should live according to Annie's rules. And Annie would certainly not approve of nights spent in some other bed.

Matt had no doubt that Joe had spent the night with Kathy. What surprised him was that Kathy should lay herself open to the angry accusations of her father. He didn't quite envisage the misery that was Kathy's daily lot – the continual whining from her mother, the constant drudgery, the cold disapproval of her father, the cheerlessness of her surroundings, the sheer physical weariness brought about by doing chores and helping with the farm. Kathy had reached the point where she snatched at happiness where she could. And for her, happiness lay with Joe.

Jim Gimbel didn't realise she'd stayed out all night that first time. But he 'caught her out', as he termed it, on the second occasion.

'Haven't you learned anything?' he shouted at her. 'I thought when you came home again that you'd learned your lesson and would lead a decent life in the future!'

'I came back because Ma needed me,' Kathy replied. 'I didn't make any promises about living like a nun.'

'Like a nun! You don't even know how an ordinary decent woman lives!'

'Don't shout at me, Dad. Shouting won't convince me.'

'You'll listen to what I say,' he ranted. 'From now on, you'll be home every night by ten o'clock –'

Kathy laughed. 'Don't be absurd. I'll do no such thing.'

'While you're under this roof, you'll do as I tell you!'

'No, I won't. I'll live my own life, and you'll accept it,' she said bravely. 'This is the twentieth century – I'm old enough to vote, to have been married, to have had a baby –'

He advanced on her, his fist raised. Her brother Martin stepped between them. 'Nay, Dad, if you hit her you'll only prove you're bigger than she is,' he said. 'Let be.'

'Get out of my way –'

'Jim, Jim,' begged his wife, 'don't carry on so! She's not doing anything worse than thousands of girls –'

'She's my daughter! I expect my daughter to behave better than those sluts –'

But he had turned away in disgust, and the danger of physical violence was over for the moment. He went about his day's work, brooding on what had happened, convinced that his only daughter was on the road to damnation. But more than his concern for Kathy's immortal soul, the affront to his own dignity loomed in his mind.

Kathy looked strained and deathly tired when she met Joe that evening. She had had to climb out of the window of her room, her father being on watch by the door in the kitchen to prevent her going out. Her skirt had snagged on a nail, she had a ladder in her tights. She was ready to dissolve in tears at the first kind word Joe said to her.

'Nay, lass ...' he said, aghast. 'What's to do? What's been going on?'

'You don't know,' she sobbed. 'You can't imagine what it's like! I'm just ... I'm just at the end of my tether, Joe!'

'You'll have to leave Holly Farm.' His voice was full of suppressed indignation. 'It's just not right –'

'I'll go back to Hotten –'

'No, Kathy, don't! Don't go away again!'

'But there's nothing else for it! If I go on seeing you while I stay at home, Dad's going to take his belt to me. I just –'

'He'd better not,' Joe said.

'There – you see? You're ready to go and have a fight with him! What good does that do? I've got to live with him, don't forget –'

'No, Kathy!'

'What?' She was taken aback by the sudden alertness in his tone.

'You just said – "I've got to live with him". But you don't.'

'But I do. It's either that, or go back to Hotten.'

'No it isn't.'

'I don't understand you –'

'Why do we keep taking it for gospel that you either have to live at Holly Farm or in Hotten? There's other places.'

'Where, for instance?'

'Beckindale.'

'Beckindale?'

Joe held her closer and stroked her hair. 'Our trouble is, we're cowards.'

She pulled herself a little away from him to look up in perplexity.

'Well, we won't face the facts, and I reckon that's cowardice,' he pointed out.

'I am facing facts,' she objected. 'If I stay in Beckindale I have to live with my father and all his funny ideas – that's a fact.'

'Nay, there's other facts. We want to be together but we're prevented because we're not married. But if we want to live together – there's nowt to stop us.' He met her gaze. 'And *that*'s a fact.'

There was a long, long pause.

'At Hawthorn, you mean?' she asked at length.

He shook his head. 'No, I've got to sell that to lay my hands on some cash. I *could* back down and go to Henry for the money but ... well ... I'd rather go ahead with the sale. But I could buy a smaller place. A little cottage in t'village, like.'

'In Beckindale?'

'Has to be Beckindale,' he explained. 'I run Emmerdale Farm. I can't do it from a long way off. And I reckon you want to be near enough to keep an eye on your Ma.'

'You ... you really mean this?'

'Never meant anything more.'

'Where in Beckindale? There's not much going.'

'Percy Edgar's cottage. You know – Demdyke Row?'

'Oh ... yes ... I know it. They're solid little places ...'

'It just came into my mind.'

'And we'd live there as man and wife?'

'Aye.'

'Could you . . . could you face t'village? And your family?'
'I could, Kathy. Could you?'
She hesitated. Perhaps even then she knew it was a more difficult thing for her than for Joe.
'Yes, I could,' she said, her chin jutting as she uttered the words.
'Well, then?'
She clung to him, suddenly eager. 'When, Joe? When?'
'Soon's I can get it going.'
'And we'll be together! Nobody to bother us!'
'It'll be great.' He picked her up and swung her round. 'It'll be just like being married.'
Perhaps they should both have remembered that they'd tried marriage, and it hadn't been much fun.

CHAPTER THREE

Joe mentioned to his mother the idea of finding another place to live. 'Hope you don't mind,' he mumbled. 'I'm looking out for a smaller house than Hawthorn – somewhere handy.'

It was in both their minds that it was odd to move into his old room at Emmerdale and then plan to move out almost at once. But it had never been Annie's habit to ask questions, and as yet Joe wasn't ready to explain his purpose.

Soon it became clear that he was interested in Percy Edgar's old house. This was in a row of sturdy cottages on the slope above the ruins of the old mill, and not far from the cricket field. He got the key from the agent, went in, and had a look round. To his masculine eye, it looked all right. Different from Emmerdale, or even Hawthorn, because out of the window you could see next door's gardens – there were houses on either side, joined on, sort of – terraced, he remembered it was called. Felt funny, having other houses squeezing up against you – like having somebody jostle you in a football crowd so as to pick your pocket!

He grinned at himself and made some attempt to estimate the attractions of the little house. It was smaller than Hawthorn, of course, and had fewer rooms. Moreover, it had been lived in by an old man, a widower, so that the wallpaper was dark in colour and even darker with age. The paintwork was drab. There was some old lino on the floors – worn and discoloured. In the fireplace in the living-room there were ashes from an old fire. Joe felt a sudden chill as he gazed at them. A life had gone from this place ...

But that was daft. Somebody had always died in an old house. It was only in a brand new place on a housing estate that you could begin absolutely fresh. And even if old Percy Edgar's ghost was hovering around, that wasn't so bad. A nice old feller, Percy – interested in everything that went on around him.

So, as it happened, were the neighbours at Demdyke Row. They saw a young man go into the old man's house, waited with interest to see him come out, and had no difficulty in recognising him as that young Joe Sugden from Emmerdale Farm. Now what was he doing, looking at a house in Demdyke? He had that old cottage up from the bridge, and the farmhouse at Emmerdale. Could it be that his mother was turning him out? What had he been up to, eh?

Joe, coming out of the front door, found himself a centre of interest from neighbouring doorways and behind lace curtains. He gave them all a dazzling, neighbourly smile, waved, and walked away.

Next time he came, he gave them even more to think about. He brought with him that Kathy Gimbel, Kathy Davis as she was now, although there was a divorce in the offing, as far as was known. Kathy Gimbel? Why was Joe Sugden bringing Kathy Gimbel to look at the house?

He unlocked the door and ushered Kathy in. The place smelt damp and neglected. Extraordinary ... Percy had only been gone a couple of months.

'You really thinking of buying this?' Kathy inquired, clearly not impressed.

'Got to buy something, now haven't I?'

'If you intend going through with it ...'

'You're not backing out, are you, Kathy?'

She shook her head and walked on into the living-room. Matters had been made worse by a fall of soot from the disused chimney. She eyed the dingy room without enthusiasm.

'Don't you like it?' Joe said.

'It makes my flesh creep.'

'Aw, that's just because it's empty. It'd be all right with a coat of paint and a bit of new wallpaper. Some shelves ...'

He made descriptive gestures with his hands.

He saw that Kathy didn't take fire at his ideas. He looked at her with perplexity. What did she want, what did she expect? They certainly wouldn't find a bijou residence for sale anywhere within reasonable distance of the farm – even if he could afford a bijou residence.

'It could look very nice,' he said lamely.

'I don't think it could, Joe.'

'But if I say no to this, Kath, it may be years before something else comes up. Property doesn't go up for sale in Beckindale very often – we're a long-lived lot.'

'I suppose that's true. How long has this been on the market?'

'Three weeks.'

'Funny it hasn't been snapped up ...'

'Nobody in the village wanting it, I s'pose.'

'But weekenders? You'd think it would be ideal for them.'

Joe hadn't thought of that. He'd been congratulating himself on having plenty of time to make up his mind, confident that no one else in Beckindale was interested in Percy Edgar's house. But folk from Bradford or Leeds – bye, they might well take one look and put down cash for it.

'I ought to show some interest to the agent,' he muttered.

Kathy studied his anxious, thin face. He was tanned from the sun but looked tired. There was so much work at the moment – harvesting was in full swing; shows were being held so that Matt was sometimes away with ewes or lambs to parade; there had been trouble with one of the milkers, there was the cricket tournament in which Joe had to play his part; he'd got himself involved in the fell race ... One thing he didn't need was a wrangle about buying property.

But it was a big step to take. Not only from the personal viewpoint: there was the money side too. Even if townies weren't after the house, the price would probably be a few thousands – prices were so high these days, and going higher. It was a lot of money to plunge with. And it wasn't really his own money, she knew. It was money belonging to the farm, from the proposed sale of Hawthorn. He didn't even have the money; Hawthorn still hadn't found a buyer.

Joe was thinking that if he made an offer for Demdyke, without consulting Henry, it would mean more trouble. Yet after all, he was manager of Emmerdale Farm. He had a right to a place to live. The company ought to provide him with living accommodation to his own taste, within reason. And it wasn't as if the money was going to disappear into a hole in the ground: he would be buying a house, which would always appreciate in value, according to Henry.

But did he want to buy *this* house? Kathy seemed so reluctant.

'I've got to go,' she was saying, making for the door. 'I've got to get to the shop – we've run out of soap powder.'

'Kathy –!'

'What?'

'What d'you think?'

She didn't turn back. 'I'm no judge, Joe. I don't know about property.'

'Oh, not that side of it. What d'you think? As a home?'

'I've got to go,' she said, and hurried out.

Her departure was noted by the neighbours. Rushing out, looking all flustered ... What could it all mean?

Another witness to her abrupt departure was Sam Pearson. He was delivering a mended work-basket to old Mrs Prentice who lived over the back at Pitcher Lane. He saw Kathy come out of the house in which Percy Edgar used to live, looking flushed and a little upset. He was interested, but not particularly bothered. It didn't begin to bother him until his daughter mentioned the place as she was giving him his elevenses. He'd asked why Joe hadn't come in for his. She replied he was down at Demdyke Row.

'What?' he said, sitting up straight so that he spilled coffee into the saucer. 'Joe's at Demdyke?'

'Yes, why?'

His lips closed in a thin line. Annie knew that look. He was distressed – angry and upset. 'What's the matter?' she asked.

'Nothing. I think I'll take my coffee out to the workshop.'
'Nay, now, Dad. Don't do that –'
'I fancy being alone,' he said. He got up, holding the coffee carefully so as not to slop any more over the side. The way he carried on, you'd think not spilling coffee was the most important thing in the world. Annie watched him, perturbed by his manner.
'When Joe gets back, tell him I'd like a word with him.'
'What about?'
'Never you mind. I'll be in t'shed.'
'Stay here, Dad. Don't go out there and brood.'
'I never brood,' he said testily. 'Can't a man have some time to himself without being accused of nonsense like that?'
Annie had been thinking quickly. 'Is it about Demdyke?' she asked. 'About Joe and Demdyke?'
'I don't want to discuss it.'
'All right, we won't discuss it. But sit down again, Dad. It's more comfortable in here – I don't want you out in t'shed sitting on an old box. You'll give yourself a stiff neck again.'
'Stop fussing ...' But he allowed himself to be soothed into sitting down in his own chair by the fire, which still showed a red glow although the day was warm. Sam liked a fire. It was comforting.
He sighed. 'Ah, Annie, Annie ... The young 'uns just rush away from us, don't they? And it's no use trying to tell 'em anything. They won't listen, don't want to listen.'
'We were the same, Dad.'
'Nay, never,' he said, very earnest. 'I had respect. So had you. Times you were hard-pressed – oh, I know, Jacob weren't an ideal husband, and there's no use saying he were. But we knew what was right, didn't we? These days ...' He shook his head. 'There's no standards any more. And Joe's like the rest – he doesn't want to listen, doesn't want to *wait* ...'
She busied herself with getting Matt's elevenses. She had said they wouldn't discuss it, so she made no reply. But her

thoughts ran on in response to her father's words.

Joe didn't want to wait. She could hardly blame him. It seemed unfair, somehow, that a mistake at the very outset should cut him off from what other men enjoyed. And yet, was it any improvement to rush into another entanglement?

She sensed that his feeling for Kathy was very strong, very genuine. She understood the protective instinct that urged him to do something to get Kathy away from her dismal parents. Oh, Annie was under no illusions. Joe wasn't looking at Percy Edgar's house with a view to living there alone.

But she kept telling herself that he would see sense. He couldn't – he really *couldn't* – go and live at Demdyke Row with Kathy Gimbel, outside the bonds of matrimony. It would be like throwing down the gauntlet to the whole of Beckindale.

Secretly she hoped the problem would be solved by someone snapping up Demdyke Row. Folk came out from the city to look at property, weekends mostly, and they must be viewing both Hawthorn and Demdyke Row. Hawthorn would cost about four times the price of the other – if somebody was looking for a holiday home, Demdyke could be quite a bargain.

But a likely buyer came on the scene for Hawthorn. A lady asked to be shown round, and as far as Annie could learn from Joe, she seemed keen.

'But it all has to go through Midgley's,' he reminded her. 'They'll let us know if she makes an offer.'

Annie hesitated. 'If she does, are you going to do anything about Demdyke?'

'I dunno.' He was about to set out for the top field with the drill, and busied himself with the connection to the tractor.

'Have you made up your mind whether to take it or not?'

'Well, I ... It's like this ... There isn't anywhere else, is there? And not likely to be.'

'That's true.'

'Thing is, I don't know whether the house could be made nice. I mean, it looks all right to *me* ...'

Annie took a grip on herself. 'Would you like me to take a look?'

Joe was surprised. He'd have thought she wouldn't want to do anything that would be a help in his removal from home. But then he thought, No, that's not Ma's way – she always plays her part, doesn't shirk anything.

'It'd be a help if you'd give me your opinion,' he said.

'When?'

'This afternoon?'

'All right. About half-past three?'

'See you there.' He got into the tractor seat and started up. Over the roar of the engine he called, 'Thanks, Ma.'

He was waiting at the door with the key when she got there in the afternoon. The neighbours on the right hand side, the Misses Carter, were gardening. They straightened as Annie walked up the path.

Annie had known them since she was a girl – Priscilla and Euphemia Carter, known as Prissie and Effie. To her, they had seemed two rather pretty, elegant girls, whom she had rather envied from her schooldays as they gadded about the dales with their escorts. Prissie had trained to be a teacher and had a good post in Hotten. Effie was a tailoress, and therefore was always rather well-dressed. In Annie's girlhood, young women in their twenties who looked well-turned-out were rather scarce. She'd admired the Carters.

Then tragedy struck. Both their parents became ill. The father's income vanished – he'd been a master plasterer. Effie gave up her job to stay at home and nurse them, on the understanding that she could carry on employment from home. But the Depression had been at its height, people weren't having clothes made privately, she couldn't get much outwork from factories. Priscilla had been more or less engaged to be married; in those days, you gave up your job if you married, and as far as Annie could recall, there were no married women teachers before the war. Because the family finances were so difficult, Priscilla put off her wedding. And put it off, and put it off, until finally her young man was called up when Hitler invaded Poland.

After that, the Misses Carter had devoted themselves to their increasingly disabled parents. Little by little they had somehow withered away. First their father died, then their mother. Now they were left, still in the little house they'd always lived in, with almost nothing to live for except gossip and whist drives.

Annie felt a little pang of apprehension as she saw them raise their heads from the dahlias they were picking. If anyone was likely to disapprove of Joe and Kathy, it was the Carters.

'Good afternoon, Effie ... Prissie ...'

'Afternoon, Mrs Sugden.' They looked at her without smiling. They didn't dislike her – you couldn't really dislike Annie Sugden. But they weren't much pleased with her. A woman church-warden! They'd been dead against it when it was suggested, and had voted against her – well, not exactly, because they'd seen everybody else was for her, so they'd just not put their hands up when the vicar said 'Those in favour?' But if anybody else had put up a hand when he said 'Those against?' the Misses Carter would have done the same.

'Lovely weather,' Annie persisted. 'Harvest's coming in well.'

'You won't be having Seeding Cut on *your* land this year, then?'

'No, I think it'll be Gimbels.'

'Ah, Gimbels.' Effie looked at Prissie, and Prissie looked at Effie. 'I see Kathy Gimbel's interested in Percy Edgar's house too,' Prissie said. 'Though why, I can't imagine. She can't be thinking of buying it.'

'I ... suppose not.'

'She was here the other day. Your father came by a few minutes later. He's doing something for Mrs Prentice, isn't he?'

Annie felt as if a shutter had been opened to let light in. So that was why Dad had been so upset the other day! He must have seen Kathy here, and when he heard Joe was thinking of buying it, had put two and two together.

Joe had gone in, leaving the door open for her. 'Excuse me,' she said, 'I better get on.'

'Chimney smokes,' Effie called after her. 'Percy always complained about it.'

Joe grinned at her as she came in. 'What were those two old biddies saying?' he inquired. 'They crane their necks so hard to see what's going on, they'll be like giraffes.'

Annie made no reply. She was looking around at the living-room. To her mind, it was a poky little place. But then, you couldn't expect palatial proportions in a terraced cottage.

'I thought of knocking down this wall,' Joe said, going into his act. 'Make it open plan . . . dining alcove . . . light paint . . .'

'What's it like upstairs?' she asked.

'Bathroom's a bit primitive . . .'

So it was. The house needed a lot doing to it to make it attractive. She really felt that it was too much work for a busy farmer.

She suggested as much to Joe, who shrugged. 'Nothing else available, though, is there?'

'You could stay on at Emmerdale until something better came up.'

'But Ma . . .' He coloured. 'You can't live a life of your own there. Grandad's always on at me.'

'He spoke to you, did he?'

'It's not his business,' he said hotly. 'I don't know why he –'

They heard a voice downstairs. 'Anybody home?' It was Henry Wilks. He came halfway up the stairs so that his balding head was visible from the little landing. 'Matt told me you were here. What do you think, Annie?' He came up to the landing and peered into the bathroom. 'Ooh . . . A bath like that, with claw legs! Practically an antique.'

'Ma isn't taken with it,' Joe said.

'I didn't say quite that, Joe. It's all right for somebody that's got the time and the energy to carry out improvements.'

'What are they asking?' Henry wanted to know.

'Five thousand.'

Henry drew in an audible breath. 'You'd have to spend another couple of thousand on modernising it. Seven thousand ...'

'That's not much these days, Henry.'

'Not if it's what you really want, Joe. Don't you think you could wait for something more suitable?'

'Do you say it would be a bad buy?'

'No-o ... You'd have to pay ten or twelve thousand for the same sort of place in a town. It's worth the money in a way.'

But Joe was downcast. Standing here with two sensible people, who didn't like the look of the house, he felt a fool. And Kathy didn't like it. And he really didn't have much inclination for refurbishing it. And five thousand could be used to better purpose. And ... well ... he'd gone off the idea.

That lasted until he saw Kathy again. She'd been having a bad day at Holly Farm, and by contrast Demdyke Row seemed a haven of peace. When Joe reported his mother's opinion and Henry's, she sighed. It seemed Joe had turned against the idea. What a pity.

'I didn't think it was all that bad,' she murmured.

'Didn't you? But I thought ...'

'Oh, well – you know how it is, Joe. I was down in the dumps anyway. And Demdyke reminded me of the flat I started my married life in. Rotten, it was.'

'There you are. You don't like it.'

She linked her arm in his, suddenly much more confident than he was. 'If it was done up nicely, I might deign to call on you there.'

'You mean it?' he cried. 'You'd really go along with it?'

'Why not!'

As far as Joe was concerned, that settled it. He decided to

ring the agent first thing in the morning to make an offer. But he was forestalled by the agent ringing him to report that the lady who had seen Hawthorn last Sunday had suggested a price of fourteen-and-a-half thousand for it.

'Fourteen-and-a-half?' he said. 'But I thought we were supposed to get sixteen?'

'Might do,' Mr Midgley said, tapping the table as he spoke. 'If you hang on for a bigger price, you might well get it. But autumn's coming on, folk don't do much house-hunting once the weather turns bad. You might have to wait until spring before anybody actually take an interest. Don't forget, property in the dales always looks more lonesome in winter. It puts folk off.'

'Yeah,' Joe said. He thought about it. 'I'll come in and discuss it.'

He rang the Woolpack, but Henry had already gone out to spend the day in Harrogate with a lady friend. Amos refused to say when he might be back. 'Never tells me owt,' he sniffed. 'He's afraid I'll put it in the *Hotten Courier* as part of my work as local reporter, I suppose.'

'Will you tell him when he gets back, I'm going to see Midgley this afternoon.'

'He won't likely be back till after teatime.'

'Oh, heck. All right, tell him anyway. I'll catch up with him by and by.'

Joe had no experience of property dealing. When Jamieson's land was added to Emmerdale, Henry had taken care of all the legalities, and when the freehold of Emmerdale was obtained from Verney's, that too had been a company matter. Private dealing in houses was beyond Joe.

But the principle must be more or less the same as dealing in livestock. You looked at the item, made up your mind about the price you were prepared to go to, and made an offer. The client who wanted to buy Hawthorn had reached this stage. Joe thought about the offer as he drove to Hotten and decided it was best to take it. If they waited for a larger sum, months might go by. In that case, they wouldn't have the use of the money and the house would be standing empty, deteriorating a little as empty houses do. They might not actually get a larger price even if they waited. And meantime they did need that trailer.

And Joe wanted to make an offer for the house in Demdyke Row. If he didn't take the offer on Hawthorn, he wouldn't have the money to buy Demdyke.

As far as he could see, the *pros* outweighed the *cons*.

He was surprised to find that the estate agent had the prospective buyer waiting to talk to him when he arrived. 'Mrs Collins,' he introduced her. 'Owns that chain of boutiques – perhaps you've seen the one in the Bull Ring? Magenta, they're called.'

'Well, no ... can't say I have. How d'you do.'

'How d'you do, Mr Sugden. I'm very taken with your cottage.'

'Aye, I thought you fancied it when you looked round it.'

'Thing is, Mr Sugden, I don't have time to mess about. I'm offering for Hawthorn, but I don't want to be gazumped. What d'you say?'

'Gazumped?'

'That's ... er ... a term that means agreeing to one offer and then accepting a higher one.'

'Oh, I wouldn't do that,' Joe said, shocked.

'You'd be surprised,' said Mrs Collins. She was a middle-aged lady, very competent and dressed in clothes a little too trendy for her, but smart. 'I've had it happen once already this year. Now, I'm prepared to go right ahead with buying Hawthorn – sign a contract straight away. What d'you say?'

'Contract? When?'

'Today.'

'Oh, no,' Joe said. He looked from Mrs Collins to Midgley. This was some kind of plot. Things were going too fast.

Midgley glanced apologetically at Mrs Collins. 'If you'll allow me a word in private with my client?' he suggested. Mrs Collins nodded, got up briskly, and marched out.

'It's genuine,' Midgley said. 'I've been into it – spent yesterday afternoon checking. She's anxious to get a house so she can have it ready to invite her family for Christmas. They're abroad – son and daughter-in-law and two kids. She'll want some work done on the house so she wants the contracts signed. You needn't have any anxiety about it if you go ahead. But you've got to decide now. If you pussyfoot, she'll go elsewhere. She's looking at a place in Rydale as well.'

Joe asked all the sensible questions he could think of but it all came down to the same thing. He had to make up his mind here and now to accept or reject. He asked for an hour to go and speak to the family solicitor, who had handled his father's will and the other minor matters of Emmerdale until Henry came on the scene.

Mr Schofield was prepared to get things moving if Joe really wanted it. 'If you're satisfied,' he said in his gloomy voice, looking at him over his specs.

'Aye ... I reckon it's on the square. I'll go ahead.'

'Just as you say,' Schofield said, looking as if he'd heard the Bank of England had crashed.

The result was that before Midgley's closed for the day, Joe had signed a contract for the sale of Hawthorn, shaken hands with Mrs Collins, and then after her departure made an offer for the house at Demdyke Row.

'Um ... ah ... I have a prior offer on that,' Midgley said. 'I'll have to speak to the executors of Mr Percy's estate.'

'What's the offer you've got?'

'The same as yours – five thousand.'

Joe hesitated. 'Who's offering?'

'I'm not at liberty to tell you that, Mr Sugden.'

'Tell me this, at least. Is it somebody from outside Beckindale?'

'Ah well, yes, I can reveal that. Yes, the client comes from Birmingham.'

'I see. A holiday home, is it?'

'I imagine so.'

Joe felt he was exonerated from blame if he put in a higher bid. He wanted the house to live in, not to visit for a few weeks each year. 'I'll offer five and a quarter,' he said.

'Um ... I'll inform the executors, Mr Sugden. But they may have made up their minds to take the first offer.'

'Can't I gazump them?' Joe grinned.

'I really prefer not to use that word,' Midgely said primly.

'Whatever word you use, I've made a higher offer so they ought to be more interested in me. When will I hear?'

'Tomorrow, some time.'

'Great.'

Joe went home, rather pleased with himself. He'd done a stroke of business rather after the Henry Wilks style – in one fell swoop he'd contracted to sell Hawthorn and made an offer for Demdyke.

But Henry seemed singularly unimpressed when he reported it all to him. 'You do understand,' he said, 'that even though you've signed the contracts, the money won't be in your hot little hand for ages yet?'

'How's that?' Joe said, a bit put out.

'Well, the legal side's been done so quickly that as soon as they can, the solicitors will want to go over everything comma by comma – and *then* they'll pass on the money.'

'That doesn't seem fair! If I fell in with Mrs Collins's wishes, her solicitors ought to cooperate –'

'Oh, you'll get the money all right. But all I'm saying is that it won't be tomorrow, nor yet the next day.'

'But you do think I was right to close with the offer?'

'Not much use saying no, now it's done, is there?'

'You in the huff, Henry?'

'Not a bit,' Henry said, frowning a little. 'You said you wanted to stand on your own feet, and now you're doing it. With a vengeance.'

'All right,' Joe said, stiffening. 'If you won't give an opinion, that's okay. Only don't bring it up afterwards and say I should've consulted you. I tried to – you'd gone to Harrogate.'

Henry's frown deepened. 'I take your point,' he said in a very cool tone.

Matters didn't improve for Joe when Midgley got in touch again. 'It's like this, Mr Sugden. I reported your offer to the executors, who felt duty bound to inform the first would-be buyer. That person has increased his offer to the same sum. You're both offering five and a quarter.'

'That's daft,' Joe said. 'What's point of that? Why didn't he offer five and a half?'

'Because he feels five and a quarter is as much as he wants to put out on a weekend cottage.'

'So where does that leave us?'

'I've talked it over,' Midgley said with a sigh. 'The agreement is that the first client to settle shall have the house. So it's up to you now. Do you wish me to go ahead and say you will put down a deposit and settle quickly?'

Joe thought fast. The money would be coming from the sale of Hawthorn, but not immediately. However, the bank would lend him five thousand on the strength of the contract signed for Hawthorn. He was sure he could get a bridging loan; he'd got quite a good relationship with the bank manager.

'Okay, go ahead,' he said to Midgley. 'What deposit do you need?'

'Ten per cent. I should want the cheque for that today, as earnest of your firm intention to go ahead.'

'I'll bring it in immediately after midday.'

'Very well.'

Five hundred and twenty-five pounds deposit. The cheque would empty the current account of Emmerdale Farm. No harm in that – there would be stock sold at Loudwick Market day after tomorrow which would put some of it back, and he could put in the small amount from his personal account.

He smiled somewhat ruefully. Quite the wheeler and dealer, wasn't he! If this was what Henry went through every day of the week, he could keep it. It was enough to give you stomach ulcers.

He finished up as fast as he could on the top field and after a quick wash and change, hurried to Midgley with the cheque for the deposit. He then went to the bank and chatted up the manager.

'I'll have to let you know,' Harrison said.

'Aw, come on, Mr Harrison. You've given me credit before now –'

'But that was for the fencing so you could go certificated. And it wasn't for a sum as large as this.'

'Yes, but –'

'It's quite likely you'll get it,' Harrison soothed. 'But I have to get verification from head office.'

Joe went home, the stomach ulcers showing every sign of becoming a reality at the suspense. Just before the office closed for the day, Midgley rang to say that his offer was accepted – he was now expected to go ahead with the purchase of the house in Demdyke Row. If anything went wrong now, the deposit would be forfeit.

'Oh, heck,' groaned Joe.

Kathy couldn't make out what was wrong with him that evening. He thought it best not to tell her the ups and downs of the negotiation – after all, why bother her with something she couldn't influence? She said at last, 'Are you angry with me Joe? Have I done something?'

'You? Of course not –'

'Because if it's about what I said over at Demdyke, I want you to know I see it all different now. I think it can be made into a lovely little home.'

'Oh, Kathy!' Despite the fact that they sat in full view of everybody in the Woolpack, Joe leaned forward to plant a kiss on her lips.

Well, there, thought Amos, studying them through the wineglass he was polishing. If the *Hotten Courier* went in for a gossip column like that there Nigel Teamster in the *Mail*, this would make a juicy item . . .

If he had but known it, juicier items were to follow.

Annie called Joe in to the phone the next morning. 'It's

the bank,' she told him as he hurried in from the barn. She half-expected him to tell her what it was about, but he simply went by, looking rather white.

And even whiter when he put the phone down. The bank manager had had bad news. 'I'm really sorry, Mr Sugden. But credit's tight at the moment. Head office turned it down.'

When Joe got back to the sacks of feed he was unloading, Matt left him in peace for some minutes. Then he said, standing straight with a hand in the small of his back, 'Hey-up! Getting old, I am. Let's have a breather.'

'Oh, let's get on with it!'

'You're heaving feed about like Hercules,' Matt said. 'Anything wrong?'

'Nowt as you'd notice.'

'What then?'

'The bank's turned me down. I wanted a loan for buying Demdyke Row.'

'But you've got the money,' Matt said in astonishment. 'From Hawthorn.'

'Nay, that doesn't come to hand for weeks, from what I can make out.'

'Well, you can put off buying Demdyke until then.'

Joe explained the dilemma he was in. 'Worst of it is, I'll lose the deposit.'

'By the holy, that's a blow, isn't it!' Matt wandered to the door of the barn and stared out at the view. To him, the thought of seeing over five hundred pounds disappear was unthinkable. He'd never had five hundred to play about with.

After a moment the solution came to him. 'You could ask Henry,' he pointed out.

'Nay.'

'What d'you mean? Henry's got the money. You need it.'

'Henry and me have had a tiff. He's not fond of me at the moment.'

Matt stared at him. 'Don't be daft.'

'It's not daft. It's fact. Henry's annoyed with me.'

'What have you done?'

Joe groaned. 'Been tactless,' he said. 'Damned tactless, if you want to know. It's like them nature films on telly – young buck challenging the old one. I just barged on, trying to show him he wasn't the big high panjundrum. And he let me do it, knowing I'd come a cropper. And I have.'

Matt came and sat down beside his brother-in-law on the sacks of feed. 'Listen,' he said in his slow, quiet way, 'Henry doesn't bear a grudge. I think you've got it all wrong.'

'You're not one to see bad in anybody,' Joe sighed. 'But Henry's got his share of pride, and I hurt him. He'd be tickled to death to see me crawling back with my tail between my legs.'

'That's it, is it, then?' Matt asked. 'It's not Henry that's the problem. You don't want to eat humble pie.'

'Would you?' Joe demanded.

Matt grinned suddenly. 'To save losing five hundred quid? You bet!'

Joe glared at him, then began to laugh. 'You've got a point,' he said. And after a moment added: 'It's not just losing the deposit. It's losing the cottage. I've more or less promised Kathy I'm getting it.'

Matt ran a hand up and down the edge of a paper sack where it was stitched. 'Is that what it's about, then?' he said. 'You and Kathy?'

Joe said nothing.

'Hm-m ... Well, there's nobody else with that kind of money except Henry. If you're really a sensible businessman, you've got to go to whoever has the finance. Or at least, that's what I'd have thought.'

'Yeah,' Joe said. He got up. 'Can I leave you to finish this while I go to see if humble pie's on the menu?'

Joe went in search of Henry. He found him in the village shop, looking over the books. 'Can you spare me a minute, Henry?'

Henry closed the stock ledger and waved him to a chair. 'What can I do for you?'

'You can lend me five and a quarter thousand.'

'Eh?' Henry said, startled.

'You like me to hand it out straight. That's what I'm doing.' Joe explained his predicament. 'You'll get it back, soon's I get the money for Hawthorn. But for the moment, I'm stuck.'

'Suppose I say I can think of better ways of using my own money?'

'I wouldn't blame you. I've gone about this wrong. I see that now. And Matt said . . . Well, the long and short of it is, I've got to come cap in hand to you. And I feel that I ought to have done that in the first place, instead of trying to do it all off my own bat.'

A long pause ensued. Joe saw that Henry wasn't minded to let him off scot free.

'All right,' he said at length. 'I'll lend you the money to buy Demdyke. But only at the same interest as you'd pay to the bank.'

'What?' Joe jerked out.

'I don't see why I should lose money by lending it to you interest free.'

Joe looked at him. 'All right.'

'Good. I'll post-date this cheque seven days,' Henry said, taking out his cheque book and unscrewing a gold fountain pen, 'so as to give the solicitor time to draw up a proper contract. The deeds for the property are to be deposited with *my* solicitor until the debt is completely cleared.' He glanced up at Joe. Joe nodded. Henry went on with writing the cheque. 'And you pay all the costs of the agreement.'

Another pause. Henry straightened and looked at Joe. Young dark eyes met middle-aged blue eyes. There was a touch of steel in both.

Joe nodded. 'I see I'm getting a lesson as well as the money.'

'It's always a good idea to learn while you can, Joe.' Henry signed the cheque, tore it out and handed it over. He held out his hand. 'Shake to seal the bargain?'

For one moment Joe felt like telling him to drop dead.

But then he recalled his own phrase, about the young buck challenging the old one. After all, he was to blame. It was only right that Henry should flourish his antlers a little.

Joe took his hand. Henry suddenly smiled. 'You're not really losing, you know, Joe. I'd say we've come out about even.'

'Think so? You're the one with the money on your side,' Joe said in rather a glum tone.

'Aye, but you're the one with youth on your side.' Henry shook his head at him. 'You don't know how lucky you are, lad!'

Joe was in two minds about that when he got home again. He'd seen Midgley, committed himself irrevocably to the buying of Demdyke Row, and to whatever that entailed. It was what he'd wanted – wasn't it?

Why didn't he feel ecstatic about it, then?

His mother had kept his tea hot for him. Matt had gone out for a date with Lucy Stubbs, Sam was at work in the shed. 'Have you told Kathy you've settled it?' she asked.

Joe looked up, surprised. It was the first time his mother had actually named Kathy in regard to Demdyke Row.

'Not yet,' he said. 'I'm seeing her later if she can get out.'

She took away his dirty plate and brought the pudding. Then she sat down opposite him, the oven cloth still in her hands.

'Joe,' she said in a very serious tone, 'I haven't asked what you're planning, but I'd be a fool not to have some idea. Don't think I'm unsympathetic. I know what it must seem like to the pair of you – sort of suspended –'

'You don't know, Ma. You can't.'

'Oh, you'd be surprised how much I recall of what it was like to be young, Joe.' She paused a moment, her thoughts going back to some moments of crisis in her own youth. Then she went on, gathering her courage to say it: 'There's one thing you may not have thought of. You've been blinded by your own impatience, happen. You haven't –'

'Not blinded. I know what I'm doing.'

'Let me finish, lad. Call it by some other name if you want, but I think it's lack of patience. It may take you into a situation you'll find hard, Joe. You've always had plenty of friends in Beckindale – have you thought what it might be like if folk turned against you?'

'I don't care about other people –'

'So you say. But look before you leap, Joe. It's very easy to put people against you in a village. It's not so easy to win respect again.'

He had too much on his mind to listen to his mother. Besides, he felt that he and Kathy deserved some happiness. If the rest of the world didn't like it, too bad!

CHAPTER FOUR

Annie held her peace for the next two weeks. She was kind and helpful about the cottage, measuring up for curtains and making them on her own sewing machine. She provided a rag rug for the living-room, although she'd intended to give it to the Bring-and-Buy Sale.

Matt helped to ferry the household goods from Hawthorn to Demdyke. He too was uncritical in his manner. To be accurate, there was nothing as yet to be critical about. Joe had not actually announced that he and Kathy were to make their home together at Demdyke. But everyone knew it at Emmerdale, and not everyone was as calm in viewing it as Annie and Matt.

Old Sam was very bitter. He couldn't speak to Joe without blame in his voice, couldn't look at him without censure in his eyes. Joe had expected that, and never responded with annoyance. He knew he was hurting the old man; it was up to him to bear all the hard words that his grandfather directed at him.

Henry Wilks was careful to have no opinion on the matter. He had seen more of the world than Annie or Sam, and wasn't the least bit shocked by Joe's plan. But he was worried by it. Having owned the village shop for some time now and played quite a part in running it, Henry knew what the women of the village thought and felt. He wondered if Joe had any conception of how conventional they were. As for the men, they could be divided into roughly three groups: those who would be carefully neutral like himself, those who would disapprove like Sam, and those who would be in the 'nudge-nudge-wink-wink' category. Henry felt that the first group would be rather small . . .

The day came when Joe had to take the plunge. He said to his mother: 'We'll be moving into Demdyke on Friday, Ma. I've finished the painting, more or less.'

She gave him the opening he needed. 'We?'

'Kathy and me. But you knew that.'

She nodded.

'Wish us well, Ma.'

'I do – you know that, lad. But you'll need more than good wishes.'

'I . . . I didn't come out with it till now because I knew you disapproved –'

'That's not –'

'Wait, I'm trying to explain. I wasn't afraid of your disapproval. It's just that I didn't want us to have a row, like Dad and Jack when he was trying to live his own life.'

'I see.'

'I sort of let you get used to the idea . . . Bit by bit . . . But the time's come to stand up and be counted. Kathy and I are going to live together like man and wife because that's how we feel about each other. It just isn't fair for us to be unhappy and hanging about waiting for the divorce. It makes no sense.'

'What you're doing will make no sense to Jim Gimbel.'

Joe smothered a groan. 'I'm going to see him this evening. Kathy wanted to tell him on her own, but I didn't think that would be right.'

Or even safe, thought Annie. Jim could be violent at times. He'd once actually attacked Joe, over a fiddling matter of some strayed sheep.

'I'll speak to him, if you like,' she offered.

'Nay. It's my job to do that.'

But he wasn't looking forward to it. He met Kathy by arrangement in the Woolpack 'for some Dutch courage', as he said with a grin. But neither of them made any headway with their drinks.

'I'm dreading this,' Kathy muttered.

'I'm not so keen on it myself.'

'Mebbe we should just drop it, Joe.'

'What, living together?' His head came up. He stared at her in utter dismay.

'Nay, love.' She put her hand over his on the table. 'Nay, never that. It's the only thing that's kept me going these last weeks. Things at home became even worse a couple of weeks ago. It was as if Dad were showing me how much I wanted to get away from him.'

'You should have told me –'

'No, no – we had enough on our plates. And as if that wasn't bad enough, Ma took it into her head to argue on Martin's side about making a move towards getting attestation. She's always been in favour, but she couldn't have chosen a worse time ... When he shouted her down, she took to her bed again.'

'Oh, Kathy! Poor lass!'

'She's up and about again now. It was just a bit of acting. Then Davey asked if he could go out and get a job in Hotten, instead of having to learn farmwork. I can tell you, that row lasted two days. No, no, Joe, if it was only to get away from my family – if I didn't love you, even – I'd leap at the chance of living at Demdyke Row.'

'But you do love me.'

'Aye, I do, Joe. And that's why I'm never going to go back on what we're doing.'

'So what did you mean about letting it drop?'

'Let's just move into Demdyke and let Dad pick the bones out of that.'

Joe was tempted. Not to have this confrontation that was looming ... Then he sighed and squared his chin. 'Nay, it's got to be done. It isn't honest if we don't. But you don't have to come, lass. I'll go and see him by myself.'

She squeezed his hand. 'As if I'd let you.'

'I mean it. It might be better.'

'You mean he wouldn't have a target to shout rude names at.' Her tone was hard and angry, but as she went on her voice cracked. 'Oh, Joe, why can't he be like your Ma?'

'There's only one like her,' Joe said.

They drove up to Holly Farm. Dusk was falling. The old stone house looked mellow, even picturesque in the shadows. On the slope above, the white shapes of sheep moved like solid ghosts. Everything was peaceful.

Kathy led the way in. Her mother had sided the dishes after the evening meal, Martin had gone out to a darts match at the Malt Shovel, young Davey was upstairs gluing a model aeroplane together, and the master of the house was frowning over some expensive new scheme for improving egg production reported in *Farmers' Weekly*.

'Hello,' Kathy began with inane brightness. 'I've brought Joe along. He's got something to tell you.'

Jim Gimbel folded his paper and put it by. He looked without welcome at the visitor. He didn't like his daughter being friendly with men; she was a married woman. It was worse still if she was friendly with married men. And Joe Sugden was no favourite at the best of times.

'Come in, come in,' chirped Freda Gimbel, trying to make up the lack of hospitality. 'Sit down, Joe. Would you like a cup of tea?'

'I'll stand, thanks,' Joe said. 'Mr Gimbel, I've got something important to say.'

'Important to who?' Jim asked.

'To all of us. It's about Kathy and me.'

Jim's eyes went from Joe to Kathy and back. He sensed the tension in their attitude. He got up from his chair.

'What can you want to say to me about my daughter?' he wondered.

'It's quite simple. Kathy and I are moving into the cottage I've just bought in Demdyke Row.'

In a way, Jim's surprise came as a shock to Joe. The move had been foreshadowed so long at Emmerdale and become so much an accepted thing that he'd somehow imagined Jim would be more or less prepared.

But he was wrong.

Jim gave a great gasp, as if he'd been hit in the stomach.

He stepped back, almost staggered. Behind him his wife gave a strange little cry.

'I thought it was only right to come and tell you, Mr Gimbel. There's nothing wrong in it ... nothing ...' Joe searched for a word '... nothing dishonourable. As soon as the divorce comes through, Kathy and me'll be wed.'

'No!'

It was a great shout of rejection. It seemed to fill the kitchen, to echo up through the house. Above, there was a sudden sound – young Davey starting to his feet in alarm.

'It's settled, Mr Gimbel. It's no good saying no. We're moving in tomorrow.'

'My daughter going to live with a man outside wedlock –'

'Kathy,' moaned Mrs Gimbel, 'how could you? The disgrace ...'

'It's no disgrace, Mrs Gimbel,' Joe said. 'Everybody in Beckindale knows how we're placed. I'm married to a girl who's filing for divorce on grounds of breakdown of the marriage. Kathy's married to a chap who cleared out almost at the start. In a few months we'll both be single again. Then we'll –'

'By God, you won't!' Jim shouted. 'I forbid it! Kathy, go up to your room.'

'No, Dad, I'm staying. This is –'

'Do as you're told! Out – this minute!' He pointed to the door, looming over her like a furious pillar that might fall on her.

'Don't speak to her like that,' Joe said, taking Kathy's arm and pulling her to his side, but a little behind him. 'I regard her as my wife. You can't treat her like that.'

'You hold your tongue!' Jim roared. 'Young whippersnapper – walking in here, telling me you intend to drag my daughter down still further –'

'Don't be so daft! Kathy's not been dragged down –'

'You think not? Caught in fornication –'

'In what? Dear heaven, where did you get that word?'

'In the Bible – but you're little acquainted with the Bible, for all that your mother plays at being a church-warden –'

'Leave my mother out of it,' Joe said, his temper rising. 'This is atween you and me –'

'It's nowt o't'sort! You've no place in our family affairs. My daughter's reputation has been dragged in the mud far enough –'

'There's nowt wrong with Kathy's reputation except in your mind, Jim Gimbel! It's your narrow-mindedness that makes you think badly of her. You ought to be ashamed! Quoting the Bible at me? What about "let him that is without sin among you, cast the first stone"? What about "the greatest of these is charity"? But you've no charity, or else you'd be glad Kathy's got a chance for a bit of happiness –'

'No happiness can come of living in sin,' Freda broke in, sobbing with dismay. 'What will people say?'

'It doesn't matter what people say, Ma,' Kathy replied. She felt if she could get her mother on her side, perhaps in the end her father might at least accept it, although he would never approve.

'You'll find it does,' sobbed Freda. 'You're too young to know how much it hurts when people miscall you.'

'Nobody's going to miscall Kathy,' Joe declared. 'He'll answer to me if he does.'

'Answer to you?' Jim cried. 'Why, you – you *fool*! Do you think you'll impress anybody? A lad that couldn't keep his own woman, who gropes and grabs after another –'

'Now that's enough! I came to say that Kathy and me are setting a home, and now I've done it so –'

'Don't dare to walk away, Joe Sugden! I've not finished wi' thee, not by a long chalk! And don't think tha'rt taking my daughter wi' thee when tha goes –'

'I'm going, Dad. There's no use ranting –'

'Ranting? Do you think I'll sit quiet while he leads you to damnation –'

'But according to you I'm damned already,' she said bitterly. 'Fallen woman, adultress, divorcee –'

'You say the words as if they're to be laughed at! Each one's a sin – don't you understand that? I can't save you from what you've done already but by heaven I'll save you from being a public shame to me –'

'To *you*. That's it, isn't it. You're not concerned about me and my happiness. Only about how you'll look when people hear.'

'They'll hear nothing, because nothing's going to happen. You may be a whore but you're my daughter and I –'

'Dad!' Kathy gasped.

'Jim!' sobbed her mother.

'You don't want me to use the word? What else is she –'

'She's a good lass,' Joe said, putting his arm round her, 'a lovely lass, and you're sick in the head to talk to her like this –'

'Let her alone,' Jim roared. 'Take your hand off her! You're not to come near her again! I forbid you the house – you and all your family –'

'Come on, Kathy,' Joe said in disgust. He made as if to turn and leave.

Jim leapt at him. His great hand, big as a hay-rake, closed on Joe's shoulder and pulled him round. The other was drawn back for the blow.

His wife dragged at his arm. He struggled to free himself, got his arm away and was ready to strike. Joe stared at him, appalled – but determined not to have a fight.

A terrified gasp from the door brought the man up short. Davey Gimbel was staring in at them from the little passage, eyes wide with horror.

'Dad!' he whispered. 'What's going on?'

For a moment they were all frozen in silence.

'Nothing,' Joe said. 'It's all a mistake. Come on, love.' He led Kathy to the door. Gimbel's hand fell away as he moved.

'Just a minute.' His voice was thick as he spoke, as if it were a great effort for him. 'If you walk out now, you never come back into this house while I live. You're no daughter of mine. I disown you.'

'Nay, Jim, you can't turn your back on your own flesh and blood –'

'Be quiet, Freda. As God's my witness, I disown her. She's

been a grief to me ever since she passed from a child to a girl. Wayward and wicked, wicked and wayward –'

'Don't listen to him, Kathy,' Joe said, holding her close and opening the door.

'Don't talk to me like that, Dad –'

'He doesn't mean it, Kathy –'

'I do,' Jim said, his voice gathering strength again. He stood up like an Old Testament prophet, head high, shoulders squared. 'What I'm saying is the truth. I've known for years that my daughter was set on the road to shame –'

'Oh, shut up!' shouted Joe, driven beyond endurance. 'You're right round the bend, that's your trouble! Come on, Kath.' He shepherded her out with care, for she was blinded by tears.

When the door had closed on them, Jim Gimbel swung to look at his wife and younger son. 'You're my witness,' he said. 'I disown her. Her name's never to be mentioned.'

'But Jim ... Jim! Your own daughter ...'

'It's no use weeping about it, woman. You're to blame as much as anyone –'

'Me?' Freda sobbed, looking at him helplessly. 'What have I done?'

'You should have raised her better. Too soft with her – a daughter takes her views on life from her mother –'

Freda bowed her head and let the tears roll. Davey hurried over to put an arm round her. 'Don't talk to Ma like that,' he quavered to his father.

'Go to your room. This is nowt to do with you. It's nothing for childer –'

'I'm not a child,' Davey cried. 'I'm sixteen! I understand what you've been saying, don't think I don't! It's your fault Kathy –'

'My fault? My fault? That she's going to be a puppet-show to the whole village? So you're on her side, are you? Just wait, young man! Just wait till your mates start sniggering behind their hands when you walk by!'

'I don't care! Kathy's not bad!'

'Upstairs,' Jim said. He took the boy by the back of his shirt and practically threw him towards the door. 'Upstairs, and don't come down again this night. And in the morning you'll apologise for your behaviour, or you'll stay up there for the rest of the day.'

'Dad!' wailed Davey.

'Out!'

The boy scuttled off.

'Oh!' sobbed Freda. 'Oh! Heaven help me! Oh, what have I done to deserve this? Oh, my heart! I can feel it thudding –'

'Hold your tongue, Freda. Wipe your eyes and be quiet. There's nothing wrong with your heart! You're just playing up as usual, to get out of facing what's happened.' His tone was quieter now, but very hard and grim.

'Oh, Jim . . .' She couldn't stop her tears. He was unreasonable to think she could. But she tried to be less noisy, for she was afraid of him in this mood.

He sat down heavily. To do him justice, he was as hurt and sick at heart as anyone else who had taken part in the scene. He truly believed his daughter was headed straight for perdition.

'Why did it happen?' he muttered. 'I've always tried to live right. Why should I have this burden to bear?'

There was no answer. It only added to his bitterness that he felt he was unjustly punished. He closed himself away in his anger for the rest of that night, speaking not another word to his family.

Kathy took a long time to recover from the scene. She was still trembling when Joe had driven her to a quiet spot on the moors. 'What's to do now?' he murmured.

'I'm never going back there,' she said. 'Never, as long as I live.'

'You'll have to, to fetch your things, Kath.'

'Never,' she said. 'Ma can send my things, or I'll do without.'

'But what about tonight?' he said.

'It doesn't matter. I'll find somewhere.'

'You'd best come home wi' me.'

'Oh, no, Joe –'

'Yeah, of course you must, it'll be all right! Ma's taken it all in her stride. She'll give you a bed for the night.'

Kathy had dried her eyes and was in control of herself now, but she was still feeling shaky. She didn't fancy another scene. 'I don't think it's a good idea, Joe.'

'Don't be daft. We'll go and settle it straight away.' He put the Land-Rover in motion, and since she couldn't think of anything else to suggest, she acquiesced.

The family at Emmerdale had been listening to *Any Answers* on the radio. Matt was putting a patch on one of his gumboots, Sam was having a private forty winks, Annie was knitting. But the tranquil scene was at once broken up when Joe brought Kathy in. The unhappiness in Kathy was immediately obvious.

'Come in, sit down,' Annie said, springing up. To Joe she said: 'It went badly?'

'Oh, he's got his head screwed on back to front,' he growled. 'Never heard such rubbish.'

'Would you like tea? Coffee?'

Matt had given up his chair to Kathy. She had sunk down, exhausted. Joe said: 'Coffee'd be a help, Ma. And what I came for, really – can you put Kathy up for the night?'

'Eh?' cried Sam, horrified. 'Here?'

'Yes, of course, here,' said Joe impatiently. 'Her Dad's turned her out.'

'Oh, lord,' muttered Matt. He gave Kathy a glance of sympathy but she, sunk in weariness, didn't see it.

'I thought it would cause a storm,' Annie sighed. 'Milk in your coffee, Dad?'

'Milk, coffee!' Sam snarled. 'Stop talking nonsense. Are we being asked to take in a girl that's going to do a wrong thing?'

'But she can't go home, Grandad!'

'Well, she can't stay here!'

Annie put down the cup of coffee she'd been about to

hand him. 'It's not for you to say who can stay and who can't, Dad,' she said, with unexpected sharpness. 'This isn't your house.'

'Oh, that's right, remind me that I'm only here on sufferance –'

'Now I didn't mean that and you know it. The fact of the matter is, this house is part of Emmerdale Farm Limited, and Joe is manager of the farm. If anybody says who goes and who stays, it's Joe.'

'Nay, it's for you to say,' Joe told her. 'You're head of the house.'

'There's no reason why Kathy shouldn't have the attic room –'

'But it wouldn't stop at that, would it,' Sam put in. 'Them two together under one roof –'

Kathy gave a little gasp of unhappiness. Joe glared at his grandfather. 'That's uncalled for, Grandad. I never thought you'd speak unkindly to someone in trouble.'

'I know what's right and what's wrong,' Sam said, although his voice had a quaver in it at the accusation of unkindness. 'I knew it when *I* were a lad, and it's the same now as it were then. I won't be a party to it –'

'Dad, don't get in a state –'

'*Somebody*'s got to take a stand –'

'Nay, Grandad,' Matt put in in a low tone, 'you'd not deny her a bed?'

'But *whose* bed, eh? You don't get away from *that*.'

Kathy, hearing it all through a haze of exhaustion, clambered to her feet. 'I'm sorry,' she said. 'I didn't mean to cause a row –'

'There's no row, love,' Joe said. 'It's just Grandad being –'

'Being upright!' Sam cried. 'I'm right, and you know it –'

'Let's go,' Kathy said.

'Kathy, stop where you are –'

'You stay if you want to,' she said. 'I'm going.'

She made for the door. Joe made as if to go after her then turned in appeal to his mother. 'Ma?'

'Don't blackmail your mother,' Sam cried. 'She feels the same way I do.'

'Dad, I'll answer for myself! Wait a minute, Kathy –'

But Kathy had gone out, leaving the door ajar. Joe sighed and shook his head. 'You've done a rotten thing, Grandad,' he said sadly, and hurried after her.

'I've done what's right!' Same called. But when he glanced at his daughter and Matt, they didn't show any agreement.

'Someone has to speak up,' he insisted. 'Young folk have no standards –'

'Don't go on about it, Grandad,' Matt muttered.

'But I was only –'

'Do you still want this coffee I'm making?' Annie said.

He'd never heard so much criticism in her tone in his life before. She'd always been tolerant and understanding, no matter what tantrum he threw. All at once Sam felt old and lonely. No one of his generation was at home in the world any more. It had changed ... ah, changed for the worse.

'I'll go up to my bed,' he said, getting up with stiff slowness and making his way to the door. 'I've had enough tonight. Goodnight, Annie ... Matt ...'

Joe and Kathy weren't saying goodnight. Joe had helped Kathy into the Land-Rover and sat in silence beside her for a moment.

'I'm sorry,' he muttered.

'It wasn't your fault.'

'I didn't expect that. I knew Grandad disapproved, but I didn't think he'd ...'

'It still wasn't your fault, Joe.' She pulled up the collar of her jacket. The autumn night was turning chill now. She couldn't prevent a shiver – partly from the chill, partly from dejection. 'What's to do now?'

'Only one thing, isn't there?'

'What?'

Without replying he switched on and drove quickly away. Annie, hearing the Land-Rover engine, shook her head as she set a cup of coffee in front of Matt. Joe had gone now – really gone.

Joe pulled up outside the house in Demdyke Row. At once lace curtains on the right-hand side twitched, and he knew they were watched as they walked up the path. At the doorway, Kathy tried a joke. 'Going to carry me over t'threshold?'

'Aye, love,' he said strongly, 'why not?' He picked her up and swung her into his arms. With three long strides he was in the living-room. He set her down. He kept his arms about her and stared down at her in the shadowed room. Her features weren't visible but there was the glint of tears in her eyes. Gently he kissed first one eyelid then the other. 'It'll be all right,' he whispered against her hair. 'We'll be happy, Kath.'

'Oh, Joe! Joe!'

They clung together. And then, arms about each other, they made their way upstairs.

CHAPTER FIVE

It was the sheerest bad luck that the new vicar of Beckindale, the Reverend William Hockley, came upon them first thing next morning. A keen keep-fit enthusiast, Hockley was out for his early morning jog, and took his way out from the vicarage past the school along Demdyke Row, intending to run out past the cricket field.

He saw Joe Sugden come out of a door in the middle of the row of cottages. Joe was in a hurry; it was time to be in the mistle. The two of them almost collided on the footpath outside the gate. 'Morning, Joe,' said the vicar, recalling his name from what Annie Sugden had said about the young man who was to collect her from a parish meeting.

'Morning, vicar,' said Joe and rushed on.

There was a young woman in a dressing-gown – or perhaps it was an overall – in the doorway. 'Morning, Mrs Sugden,' carolled Hockley, and jogged on to the end of the row, through the alley to the cricket pitch, and round the perimeter. He was passing the score-board when a thought occurred that made him flush to the roots of his hair. Annie Sugden had said that her son Joe was on his own at the present time, awaiting a divorce from his wife Christine.

So who was the young woman in the doorway?

Kathy had turned back into the house after the vicar's greeting, divided between ironic mirth and embarrassment. She drew the overall about her more closely. It belonged to Annie, left in the house so that if she came back to do any more cleaning for Joe it would be handy.

There was still tea in the pot. She had made it quickly for Joe, who had groaned when he saw the time. It was now quite a good cup of tea, having brewed just the right amount. She drank thoughtfully. What was she to do now?

Well, what would she have done today anyhow, the official moving-in day? She'd have to shop, for the larder was empty except for tea and coffee and powdered milk. She got a pencil and an old envelope, began on a list.

That done, she rinsed the cups and saucers, went up to wash and dress, and then, the time being half past six, she took the risk of ringing her mother from the village call box. With luck, her father would still be rinsing down.

She sighed with relief when her mother answered.

'How are you, Ma? What happened after I left?'

'Nothing much, Kathy. He never said another word all night. Hasn't spoken this morning either, except for "Pass the sugar".'

'What did you tell Martin?'

'What could I tell him? That you'd gone to live with Joe and that his father said we weren't to speak to you again.'

'Did Martin agree?'

'What do you think?' Freda Gimbel said, with a tearful note in her voice. 'He was all for packing up and leaving right then. But I persuaded him not to, for my sake.'

'E-eh, what a coil,' Kathy murmured. 'I'm sorry, Ma.'

'So'm I, Kathy, so'm I – because you know, although I've tried to stick up for you, I think what you've done is quite wrong.'

'I understand that. But you're not going to turn your back on me entirely.'

There was a strange little pause. 'Well,' Freda said at last, 'the fact is, I don't want any more trouble than I have to have, Kathy.'

Her daughter felt a little stab of pain. So it was beginning – the censure from the women. And to think that her own mother should lead the way . . .

'All right, Ma, let's not discuss it now,' she said, sounding brisk. 'Will you pack my clothes and send them on? Lucky I never brought all my things from Hotten.'

'I'll see to it. How am I to get them to you?'

Bring them, Kathy wanted to say. Bring them to me, pay me a visit. But if her mother didn't want to come, she would never force her. 'If you put them outside the door, Joe'll collect them.'

'No!' There was genuine fright in her mother's reply. 'Joe had better not set foot here, Kathy.'

'Don't be absurd, Ma –'

'I'm not! I really thought your Dad was going to hit him last night! I don't want any more trouble, Kath.'

Kathy fetched a deep breath. 'All right,' she said, 'put the case out. I think Matt Skilbeck would come and get it. Surely Dad wouldn't set about Matt?'

As she stepped out of the phone box she saw the vicar making his way to the church. Every morning since records began, the vicar of Beckindale had said morning prayers in the church – sometimes to a congregation consisting of the vicarage cat, sometimes to an empty nave. With faint blushes at the memory of his greeting to her earlier, Kathy hurried to the shop. It was too early for the place to be open for business but in a farming village the shopkeeper is always up and about the same time as its inhabitants. Kathy knocked at the side door and was rewarded by footsteps coming down from the flat. A quarter of an hour later she was on her way back with a pound of bacon, a carton of eggs, a loaf of bread, and a pint of milk.

She was putting the bacon to keep hot in the oven when the knocker went on the door. Surprised, she went through to answer it. Couldn't be the post, surely – no one knew they'd moved in yet.

It was the vicar, Mr Hockley.

'Good morning,' he said. 'May I come in?'

'Oh . . .' She glanced past him. Effie Carter was sweeping her front path, but over the broom was watching with interest. 'I suppose so, vicar, but I'm just getting breakfast for Joe.'

'I won't be a moment.' He stepped in, looking about with open interest. 'I can understand how busy you are. You just moved in, didn't you?'

'Last night. Earlier than we intended.'

'I . . . er . . . I believe I embarrassed you this morning when I went past.'

'Not particularly,' she lied.

'You're . . . er . . . Kathy Gimbel, really?'

'Kathy Davis, actually. I'm married.'

'But not to Joe Sugden.'

'No, not yet.'

'You intend to get married to him?'

'When my divorce comes through.'

'But . . . my understanding is that Joe is married too.'

'He's in the same state as me. He's waiting for the divorce.'

'I see.'

She had gone through from the living-room to the kitchen. She closed the oven door with a bang. 'You don't approve,' she said over her shoulder to him.

The vicar hesitated. 'My teaching is that marriage is for life, Mrs Davis.'

'It takes two to make a marriage, you know.'

'You're saying your husband broke up yours?'

She turned towards him, neatly folding the oven cloth as she did so, unaware of the action. 'Nay,' she said slowly, 'it never really existed. Terry walked away from it first, but I'd have gone even if he hadn't.'

'And Joe?'

'You'd have to ask Joe about that.'

Hockley sighed. 'His mother is my church-warden, you know. I've gathered that she's not very happy about all this.'

'Did she ask you to speak to me?' And then, at once: 'Nay, she wouldn't do that.'

'No, Mrs Sugden hasn't said a word to me. I'm so new here . . . And anyhow I get the impression she's not one to talk about her troubles.'

'Is that what I am? One of her troubles?'

'I didn't mean that. I'm sorry.'

She made a gesture towards the kitchen. 'You'll have to excuse me, vicar. Joe'll be wanting his breakfast . . .'

'Of course. I just wanted to say . . . Well, I'm sorry if I

blundered earlier. And though I can't approve of the situation here, if there's anything I can do to help ...'

Kathy nodded past him towards the window of the living-room. Through it, Effie Carter could be seen leaning on her broom, waiting for Mr Hockley to come out again.

'Happen you could tell folks hereabouts to remember the bit in the Bible about loving thy neighbour? That'd be a help.'

Mr Hockley didn't turn his head, but he knew what she meant. He stifled a sigh. 'That works both ways, don't forget,' he murmured. 'You have to love them.'

Kathy laughed. 'That's asking for a miracle,' she said. 'I want to be friends, but it's difficult with people who won't even open their mouths to you.'

'You've got to make allowances. This is a new situation for them ... In time I'm sure you'll find that a relationship will develop.'

'So you won't speak to them on my behalf?' she challenged. 'What's the use of offering help if you won't even do that?'

'I didn't say I wouldn't speak to them,' the vicar corrected her, his tone gentle. 'But you have to do your part.'

'Suffer in silence, you mean.'

Mr Hockley moved towards the door. 'The acceptance of suffering is one of the lessons of the church,' he remarked. 'But not many can follow the example we were given.'

'That's expecting too much, vicar.'

'I know that. I didn't say it as a reproof – we all fall short. Not just in that way, either. You know that bit in the prayers ... "We have followed too much the desires of our own hearts"?'

'Are you saying I should change my mind, go back home?'

'Well –'

'Because if you are, let me tell you my father wouldn't have me inside the door,' she swept on. 'He turned me out last night and told me I was never to come back.'

'Oh, but that was said in anger. He didn't mean it –'

'He meant it,' Kathy said. 'The day you can come to me

and tell me you've persuaded Dad to speak to me kindly, I'll go back home.'

Mr Hockley was at a loss for words. He was new in the village, didn't have any influence as yet and feared he might have little with some of those involved in this drama. Unexpectedly, he stepped up to Kathy and took her hand. 'I'm sorry,' he said. 'I'll do all I can to help. Please believe me when I say you have a friend in me.'

She was so taken aback that she couldn't reply. He was gone next moment.

Outside, Miss Carter was making little useless movements with her broom. 'Morning, vicar,' she said.

'Good morning, Miss Carter.'

'Been doing a pastoral visit?'

'Exactly.'

'Seems a funny place to see our vicar – coming out of a house like that.'

Hockley looked back at the house. He said: 'It's like all the others in Demdyke Row, Miss Carter. Architecturally, I mean.'

'I weren't speaking architecturally,' she said quickly, her faded blue eyes taking on a sparkle of disapproval. 'I meant that it's a house of sin.'

'Miss Carter!' Hockley was genuinely shocked. 'God is the judge of what is sin. You don't take that rôle upon yourself surely?'

She frowned at him, quite unabashed. 'I know what's right and what's wrong. And so should you, vicar.'

'I try to know the difference,' he said. 'But sin comes in subtle guises, you know. Arrogance, intolerance . . .'

'And it comes in open display too, vicar – broken marriage vows, for instance. No need to look around for subtle kinds, it seems to me.'

'Your view of life is simplistic, I fear, Miss Carter.'

'Simplistic? What's that supposed to mean? I'll tell you this, Mr Hockley. My sister and me, we've been churchgoers all us lives, and if vicar comes visiting we expect him to come first to folks as support him. Not giving respectability to those that flout his beliefs.'

'It seems to me that a priest, like a doctor, should go where he's needed most.'

Miss Carter gave a little gasp of annoyed surprise.

'Shall I see you in church tomorrow?' he went on, moving away from her.

'Prissie and I never miss.'

'That's good –'

'But a lot depends on how standards are kept up, it seems to me.'

'I believe,' Mr Hockley said as he turned for home, 'that you'll find God's standards are aimed at – even though we all fall short at times. Good morning.'

Miss Carter was not pleased. She went indoors to fume to her sister that the new vicar was too easy-going, and saucy with it too. 'Remember Mr Rosewell?' she demanded, harking back to the priest who had been vicar just before and during the war. 'Now *there* was a man who knew what was what!'

Prissie nodded, pouring tea for her. 'But standards don't mean anything these days, Effie. Church wants to be trendy – that's what's wrong!'

'Well, we'll see what he says in his sermon tomorrow. But if he don't speak out against what's going on right here in a respectable street like this, then I'll know where we stand.'

'Quite right, Effie. And I'll have a word with the neighbours, make sure they see it our way.'

However, the Carters found there was a certain division of interest that Saturday, because a new face had appeared in Beckindale and all the men were talking about it. Amos Brearley had taken on a new barmaid at the Woolpack.

This was almost unheard-of. The last one had been Alison Gibbons, who had moved on to keep the village shop. No one quite understood why Alison had suddenly pulled up stakes and gone, but it had had a saddening effect on Henry Wilks and, as far as one could gather, on Matt Skilbeck of Emmerdale.

People looked back on the time that Alison had been barmaid as a golden time. Mind you, that had been in the old Woolpack, before the wall cracked and the foundations crumbled, causing a hasty removal to the new premises – and you couldn't deny that the old Woolpack had been a cosier place. At least, so the older members of the community insisted.

'Used to be able to get home-made pies when Alison was there,' they mourned. 'And hot sausages, and cheese rarebit . . .'

But Amos didn't approve of that kind of pandering to public taste. In his view the Woolpack existed for the purpose of purveying beer, not fiddling little bits of things to eat. Crisps . . . he'd no objections to selling packs of crisps; you didn't have to cook them yourself, or give up your precious kitchen to a woman while she baked and grilled. Henry Wilks could say what he liked about providing food: Amos was never going to allow it in *his* saloon bar.

He wasn't even very keen on having a barmaid. He held out against the idea as long as he could. But now that he had taken on the rôle of local reporter for the *Hotten Courier* – 'stringer', it was called – he was often called out on some event in the area. And if it so happened that Henry was also out – and confound the man, he usually was! – it meant that there was no one to open the pub.

Old Walter had nearly had a heart attack about a week ago when the Woolpack was three minutes late opening. Amos didn't want that on his conscience. So when Henry returned to the attack, Amos listened – with a great appearance of unwillingness, but secretly with some relief.

'I tell you, this lass is ideal,' Henry declared. 'A friend of mine is vouching for her. She's had some experience of bar work, and wants to extend her knowledge, particularly with regard to looking after a cellar. Now you know, Amos, no one could teach her more than you could about that.'

'Aye,' Amos muttered, 'but I don't hold wi' females in t'cellar. Upsets the beer.'

Henry was about to retort that Amos himself was enough to upset even Napoleon brandy in cask, but thought better of it.

If he was going to succeed in his plea for a bar helper, it made sense not to annoy Amos. Henry didn't care whether they got a man or a woman, so long as there was someone to take over when he and Amos went out; but a director of a brewery firm had asked him, as a friend, to give this young lady a job, so Henry was prepared to plead her cause.

'You could see how she goes on,' Henry said. 'If you feel she isn't up to it, you can keep her out of the cellar.'

'It'd be best to keep her out of t'Woolpack in t'first place,' Amos grunted.

'If you guarantee never to be out when the bar is due to be opened, I'll agree.'

'But I can't guarantee that! My duties as a reporter are bound to call me out from time to time.'

'Exactly, Amos. So we need a helper.'

'I don't see that. If you could guarantee to be here when I'm out –'

'Amos, I'm not going to restrict my activities just because you suddenly see yourself as Chapman Pincher. I'll be here as often as I can, but I am *not* promising to be glued to the Woolpack in case you get called out to report a car accident.'

'But it's not suitable to have a female person living in.'

'She doesn't need to live in. In fact, this young lady's got her own transport – she'll come back and forth from Hotten.'

'Oh, indeed? Got it all worked out, have you? What's her name, then?'

'Miss Acaster, Dorothy Acaster.'

'And she's got experience?'

'She's had nearly a year in a bar in Leeds.'

'I don't want any flighty town ways here,' Amos said crushingly.

'Amos!' Henry was exasperated. 'She's a highly respectable young person with the best possible references, recommended by a personal friend of mine. What more do you want?'

Amos pondered. 'Happen it would be better to have a man,' he said.

'A man? That's no attraction! There are two men already

that folks see behind t'bar. What they want is an attractive young woman.'

'Now, Mr Wilks! I'm having no hanky panky in *my* bar!'

'Hanky panky? All she's going to do is serve beer and spirits –'

'Aye, well ... as to that ... I'd have to see. I'd rather she started by doing the tidying up and washing the glasses. It takes experience to handle the optics and that kind of thing.'

'Even if she only does the tidying up, it would be a help. You can't deny we've had our problems keeping the place going recently.'

'And whose fault is that?' Amos demanded, with a reproachful glance at his partner. 'Who went rushing out to see a business colleague in Bradford when I was out on a story?'

'And who was out on a story and couldn't be reached by telephone or any other means –'

'You can't expect telephones in the middle of the moors –'

'And you can't expect business meetings to end exactly at pub opening hours!' Wilks pulled himself together. 'Now look here, Amos – yes or no? Are we going to give this young woman a trial?'

Amos wasn't going to give an answer as easily as that. 'I'll see her,' he announced in a lofty tone.

Dolly Acaster thought Amos Brearley an odd sort of character – finicky, touchy, reluctant to commit himself in any way. But on the other hand, her quick intelligence told her that he was an undeniable expert on the handling of cellar-work. And the Woolpack was a nice little place, cosy, quiet and interesting. And Henry Wilks had sense, even if his partner seemed to have more than his share of absurdity about him.

Rather to his own surprise, Amos agreed to have Dolly on trial. She was to begin on Saturday. Dolly turned up in a dress she knew Amos would think suitable – quiet beige, high-necked and long sleeved, with no bright trimmings. She might have spared herself the trouble of dressing for the part, for all that he let her do was collect up the dirty glasses and wash them in the kitchen.

Nevertheless, her appearance was noted by the habituees of the Woolpack, and with approval.

'A gradely lass,' Bill Powers said to his wife when he got home that evening. 'Joe Sugden said to me –'

'You were never talking to Joe Sugden?' his wife Gladys cried.

'Aye, of course I were,' Bill said in surprise.

'Bill Powers, didn't I tell you that the Misses Carters and I had decided to send them to Coventry?'

'Aw, Gladys ... That's no way to treat neighbours.'

'You have to have respect to yourself,' Gladys insisted. 'This has always been a decent neighbourhood, and the sooner we let that pair know they're not wanted, the sooner they'll move out.'

'They won't move out, Glad. Joe's bought the place.'

'Well, he can sell it again. And the sooner the better.'

'But what harm are they doing?' Bill protested. 'She's a quiet enough girl, so far as I can see. I mean, she's not exactly the scarlet woman.'

'Oh, you don't understand,' his wife said. 'You're off all day in that office in Hotten – you don't see her flaunting herself –'

'She hasn't had much time for that, has she? She only moved in last night.'

'She was out pinning washing on the line this afternoon.' Gladys sniffed. 'Skimpy, that's what her ... her garments are.'

'Gladys,' groaned her husband. 'You're not going to say a girl's evil because she wears see-through nighties?'

Glady put her hands over her ears in horror. 'Bill Powers! Don't you dare talk about such things! You seem to forget – she's not married to that man!'

'I'm not forgetting it –'

'I want it firmly understood that we don't speak to them. We've got to make a stand against this sort of thing. We've all agreed – everybody in Demdyke Row.'

Bill made a grunting noise which she took for agreement.

But privately he was thinking that no amount of disapproval from Gladys was going to make him turn his back on a long-standing friend in the Woolpack.

He comforted himself by thinking that time would settle it all. In a month or so, the neighbours would be completely tolerant of the young couple next door.

He was wrong there. The weeks turned into months, and autumn turned into winter and then winter into early spring – but still the icy disapproval of the inhabitants of Demdyke wasn't melted. The Reverend William Hockley could preach sermons about charity and brotherly love, but no one took it to themselves. Even in Joe Sugden's own family, the disapproval didn't fade.

His grandfather was stern in his condemnation. The day Joe and Kathy set up home together, old Sam went out without his breakfast and was missing for most of the day, nearly driving his daughter to the point of reporting his absence to the police. It was Matt who brought him home at last, quite ill with exhaustion. He'd been up in a disused shepherd's hut beyond Grey Top, stubbornly determined not to come home while Joe insisted on 'living in sin' with Kathy Gimbel.

'Come on now, Grandad,' Matt said in a gentle but firm tone. 'You're not punishing Joe by doing this. You're punishing Ma.'

'She's to blame too,' Sam burst out. 'She should tell him to behave properly!'

'Joe's a grown man, Grandad. Ma can't order him about.'

'She could show disapproval! She doesn't even reprove him!'

'How d'you know?' Matt asked. 'You haven't always been there when Ma has been talking to Joe.'

'Then he's defying her – and that's wrong. "Honour thy father and thy mother, that thy days may be long upon the land –"'

'Aye, days are long upon the land, and you're not making them any easier by acting up like this. You're not being fair, Grandad.'

'Me? Not being fair?' The old man was aghast.

'Joe's got the farm to run. You're adding to his worries by going missing –'

'I never thought I'd see the day when Emmerdale would be in the hands of a man who'd behave like this –'

'Joe's the manager of Emmerdale Farm. There's nothing you can do about it. Think on, Grandad. Joe is the mainspring of our lives. What he does, what he decides – that's what makes the difference between success and failure wi' Emmerdale.'

'Are you saying I should condone evildoing just because Joe runs the farm and I live there?'

Matt took the old man by the elbow and steered him out into the cold night air. 'Nobody asks you to condone it, if it *is* evildoing –'

'You mean you don't think it's wrong?'

'Nay, my mind's more on what Joe and Kathy are going through, to tell t'truth. As to right and wrong, I'm prepared to leave that to other folk that feel able to make judgements.'

'You're young Matt. You don't know what this kind of thing leads to.'

'Happen. But I do know that there's no good in making Ma even more anxious and bothered than she is already. Come on now, get in t'Land-Rover and let's get home.'

Sam allowed himself to be driven to Emmerdale. That far, he gave in. He had intended to stage a protest that would last as long as need be, to get Joe to move out of Demdyke. But he found he wasn't strong enough for that: the flesh was weak. However, at Emmerdale he kept up an unremitting disapproval of his grandson.

He was truly and deeply surprised to find himself in a minority of one. Matt ... well, it wasn't in Matt's nature to be unkind to anyone, so he wasn't taken aback when Matt continued to behave just as usual to Joe. But Annie ... Sam had expected his daughter to mount some sort of campaign to bring Joe to his senses. Instead she seemed almost to support the lad.

'You know I can't turn my back on Joe,' she objected when

he tried to make her act according to his lights. 'And Kathy is not a bad girl, no matter what you say.'

'You're helping to maintain her in her wrong attitude by allowing her to come here! Every time she comes to the house I feel it's an affront.'

'Dad, you'll not tell me who I can or can't invite to this house.'

'Are you saying that if it came to a choice, you'd side with her?'

She put down the iron and came to stand by his chair. 'You wouldn't force me to make a choice, would you?' She laid a hand on his shoulder. 'Dad, I'm not speaking here of the rights and wrongs of it – although the rules now aren't the same as they were when you were young –'

'More's the pity! There's no guiding lines any more –'

'Before the war, Dad, when I were a lass – do you remember Sally Crutchleigh, who had to leave Beckindale because she was expecting a babby?'

He shook his head, then paused. 'Aye ... little redheaded lass ... I mind her.'

'She broke her heart about it. You don't know ... you can't know ... how she cried over that one lapse. She was sent away. We never saw her again, did we?'

'Nay, she never came back.'

'And her poor mother kept pretending she'd gone to join the W.A.A.F. I'll never forget how uphappy they were, the two of them. That family was broken in two, just because poor Sally hadn't got a wedding ring. Now these days she'd be at home where she belonged, with her parents. And the babby'd have that much better start in life. You can't say it's better to break up a family – now can you?'

'That's different,' Sam objected. 'That's to do with a babby –'

'It's to do with a lad and a lass. The only reason Kathy doesn't have a child is because she uses the Pill, happen.'

'Annie!'

'You see? You've got your head in the sand! Of course

they're living together as man and wife, and of course Kathy would get with child if she didn't take precautions. Would you rather she didn't?'

'Nay ... I'm not saying that ...'

'So you're prepared to go along with one part of present-day morals but not another part –'

He bowed his head. 'I have to go along with it. I've no choice. But I don't see why you have to have the girl in the house, as if you thought it was right.'

'I'm thinking of t'family. By and by, if things go the way I think they will, Kathy will be my daughter-in-law. Does it help if meanwhile I've been unkind and unwelcoming?'

'All right. But I'll take it as a kindness if you'll let me know when she's coming, so's I can go out.'

Annie pressed his shoulder. 'And you're the one who's always saying Jim Gimbel's unreasonable. You're behaving just like him over this.'

'For once Jim Gimbel's right,' he muttered.

'Nay,' his daughter said strongly. 'He's wrong. He's heading straight for disaster, t'way he's going on.'

Not even Annie could guess how right she was. Matters in the Gimbel household were going from bad to worse.

Jim Gimbel visited his wrath on the remaining members of his household. His wife had to do as she was told and never, never refer to Kathy. His two sons had to toil all the hours of daylight on the farm. The younger boy, Davey, was too frightened of his father to do anything other than obey, but Martin Gimbel had already begun his defiance of his father over Rosemary Kendall. This young relation of the Sugden family had filled Martin's world during her stay at Emmerdale; he had even asked her to marry him. Luckily for him, perhaps, Rosemary had refused. But he had already had more than one clash with Jim over that, and so he was more prepared to stand up for himself now.

All through the winter he put up with the strict control exerted by his father; he didn't want to make things worse for his mother. But at Christmas everyone else had some fun –

there was the Christmas play in the village hall, and carol-singing. The Gimbels joined in none of this. Worse, the two boys were forbidden to attend any of the events in other households if Kathy and Joe were accepted there – and since most of the neighbouring farmers were friends with Joe, it meant the Gimbel boys were unable to attend any Christmas or New Year parties.

As February came in, the weather grew worse. The Gimbels had a bad time with lambing. Everyone was exhausted. The crisis came when Martin asked for a little money to buy a new jacket.

'What's wrong with t'old one?' Jim demanded.

'I got it soaked in Potter's Pot when I fell in day before yesterday. It's in a right mess.'

'You can take it to dry-cleaners, surely?'

'It's shrunk, Dad. I can hardly get into it now.'

'You hung it too close to t'stove when you were drying it,' his father said. 'You'll know better another time, won't you?'

'I won't fall into Potter's Pot again, especially if I get a sheepskin coat.'

'You're not getting a new jacket so don't think it.'

'But Jim,' Freda put in, 'he really needs one. He's really grown out of that old one – and it's right thin, anyhow.'

'You can knit him a sweater to wear under it, then.'

'I'm not putting on any more layers of clothes,' Martin declared. 'I can hardly bend my arms as it is, I've got so many sweaters on under that coat.'

'If you were working hard enough, you wouldn't need 'em –'

'Nobody can say I don't work hard,' Martin cried. 'That's not fair –'

'Nay, Jim, the lad's right –'

'You hold your tongue, Freda. I'm speaking to my son. You'll do a day's work like me, and you'll wear the jacket you've got like me, and we'll have no rubbishing talk about sheepskin coats –'

'Damn it, Dad, other men have proper gear –'

'Don't you use foul language to me, boy –'

'Foul language? I only said damn it –'

'Just because your sister's lost her sense of right and wrong, that's no reason for you –'

'Oh, for the love of Pete! Don't drag Kathy into *this* too –'

'Perhaps you think we should forget it? Perhaps you think we should live the way she does, a shame and a disgrace –'

'Look here, Dad, all I'm doing is asking for money for a new jacket, not getting started on a moral tract –'

'I've told you, you'll get no money from me for foolish luxuries –'

'A decent coat isn't a luxury! All right, so I don't get a sheepskin – but I need *something* –'

'That's enough. I've told you my decision.'

'You mean I'm not allowed to argue against anything you say? That's dictatorship!'

'I'm the head of this house and you'll do as you're told.'

Martin turned to the door, walked out, and slammed it behind him. His father rushed after him. 'Martin! Martin, come back this minute and close the door quietly!'

'Drop dead,' Martin said, and stalked off.

He didn't come home until very late that night, and refused to give any explanation of where he had been. If his father had but known it, Martin had only come back to collect a few of his personal possessions. As soon as he could get out of the house without being noticed, he did so. He hitched a ride on a lorry into Manchester. The note he left explained everything. 'I've had enough. I'm signing up with the Royal Engineers. Love to Ma, from Martin.'

Freda Gimbel wasn't even allowed to see it. Her husband happened to come in first and found it on the kitchen table. He threw it straight on the fire.

CHAPTER SIX

Kathy heard nothing of these events until almost a week later, when Martin wrote to her from his training depot. 'I expect Ma's been in touch to let you know I've left,' he wrote, 'but this is to let you know I'm fine and settling in okay. The camp is quite comfortable . . .' And so on, for a page and a half.

Kathy was stricken. Her mother had not contacted her at all. She'd no idea what had happened.

Joe came home at midday for his dinner, to find her moving about like an automaton. 'What's up?' he asked in concern. 'Them next door been getting at you again?'

For answer, she handed him Martin's letter. He read in silence. Then he said, 'Best thing he could do if you ask me.'

'Joe! Think of what it must be like up at t'farm now! Dad on his own with only young Davey to help.'

'Aye.' He sighed. 'That's bad. I can't think how he's managing. He hasn't asked anyone to give him a hand, either.'

'Nay, he never will,' Kathy said. 'He'd rather die than ask for help.'

'He'll have to hire on, Kathy.'

'He hasn't the money.'

'It's daft.' Joe ate some stewed steak and potatoes, then said: 'I'll offer, shall I?'

'No, Joe, don't!'

'But it might be a way, love, mightn't it? I mean getting back to being friends.'

'Don't,' she begged. 'He'd never take charity, and least of all from you.'

'Well, Matt then. I'll ask Matt if he'd go up and offer.'

Kathy shook her head. 'He won't have anyone from Emmerdale, Joe. I don't think he'll accept help no matter who offers.'

Joe couldn't believe anyone would be so wrongheaded. A farmer had to have regard to his animals and if he needed help with them, must accept it.

'If you just stroll in, like,' he suggested to Matt, 'and see if he'd like a bit of a lift wi' the stock.'

'No problem,' Matt agreed.

But, as Matt confided to Dolly Acaster over a pint that evening, it didn't work out that way.

'Offered to set t'dog on me,' he said, shaking his head. 'I couldn't believe he really meant it, but he did.'

'He must be round t'bend,' Dolly broke out, shaking her fair head as she busied herself with the chores behind the bar. 'I've never met him. What's he like?'

'Oh, lanky, thin ... You've seen Martin? His Dad's just an older version.'

'Where's Martin, by the way? I haven't seen him in weeks.'

'Joined up, I hear.'

'What, the Army?'

'Mm ...' Matt sipped. 'Anything rather than stay at home. I recall he once told our Rosemary he'd quite fancy the Army.'

'Poor lad,' Dolly said. 'Fancy being driven from home by your own father ...'

'He's not the only one,' Matt replied.

'Aye ...' Dolly was thinking of Kathy, whom she liked a lot. Kathy didn't complain, but on the one or two occasions when Dolly dropped in at Demdyke Row, she could sense the unhappiness in her house. It was like a pall hanging over everything. And it was caused by the unbending animosity of the neighbours. As Dolly went up the path, she sensed she was being watched by the Carters; when she left, one of the old ladies was pretending to prune her roses.

'You're that barmaid from t'Woolpack?' she inquired.

'That's right. Miss Carter, is it?'

'Huh,' Miss Carter said, not deigning to reply to the question. 'That's just the kind of visitor I'd expect her to have – a *barmaid*.'

Dolly wasn't as long-suffering as Kathy. 'Why, you rotten old thing,' she said, carefully closing Kathy's gate behind her. 'I'm glad I don't have to live next door to you!'

Which did nothing to improve matters for Kathy.

Kathy rang her mother and managed to arrange a meeting with her, on a day when Freda Gimbel went to Loudwick Market. They sat together in a lorrymen's caff, drinking strong tea from thick cups and feeling miserable.

Kathy showed her mother the letter from Martin. Freda's mouth trembled. 'He didn't write to *me*,' she mourned.

'He knows it would only cause trouble. I'm sorry, Ma. I didn't realise it was going to bring all these consequences when I met up wi' Joe.'

'If you just hadn't made a public show of it,' Freda said. 'It's *that* he can't abide. He could just manage to live with the idea that you were seeing Joe, but to have you blatantly –'

'There's nothing blatant about it, Ma. If other folk'd leave us alone, we'd sink into t'background.'

'Not in Beckindale,' Freda sighed.

They parted without having gained any comfort from their meeting. Kathy's conscience was battering at her unmercifully. She felt everything was her fault, and that it was up to her to do something about it.

It took her two more days to nerve herself to it, but at length she took the road past the police cottage and the path just beyond Beckin Bridge to Holly Farm. The time was early afternoon. Her father would be coming in soon from outdoor work to make ready for milking.

Her mother was horrified when she opened the door to her. 'Kathy! What in God's name are you doing here?'

'I've come to try and sort it out with Dad. We can't go on like this, Ma! He's driving everyone away – first me, then Martin. I've got to make him see that other people have a viewpoint too.'

'Please go, Kathy. I don't want you here when he comes in. He's in a bad enough mood as it is –'

'There you are! It's not normal to have other people living

in fear of you like that. He's got to be made to understand –'

'Understand what?' said her father's voice behind her.

Kathy whirled. He had walked up from the barn, unheard by either herself or her mother in the rushing wind of March.

'Dad! I just wanted to –'

'Didn't I tell you never to come back here?' he said. His gaze on her was black, unyielding. 'Get away from here. You contaminate everything you touch.'

'But I wanted to say – you've got to listen, Dad – you've driven Martin away and you can't manage without him. You've got to come to your senses –'

'Go indoors, Freda,' he ordered.

'No, wait! Can't you see you're making her ill? She's as thin as a rail! You can't go on taking it out on everyone –'

'I don't need your opinions. Get off my property.'

'But don't you understand? The way you're carrying on, it's not normal! No sane man –'

'Don't raise your voice to me! You can't come here crying out against my views –'

'I'm only trying to explain to you that it's not right to make others suffer. Make me suffer if you must, but don't punish Ma and Martin and Davey –'

'I've no interest in Martin. He's made his bed, let him lie on it. And you – you're a stranger to me.'

'You can say that till you're blue in the face but the fact remains, I'm your daughter, Dad! You helped to make me whatever I am –'

'Don't dare to put blame to me!' he shouted. He seized her and began pushing her across the yard towards the outer gate of the farmyard. 'Get out, get away – don't come here again!'

He pushed her too fast, and she stumbled and fell on her knees, bruising herself on the stones. She couldn't help but cry out with the pain. Her brother Davey, hearing the cry from the milking shed, came running out.

He saw his sister crouched on the cobbles in tears, with his father looming over her. To his eyes, it looked as if Kathy had been struck. He rushed to help her up.

'You gurt bully!' he cried at his father. 'Let her alone –'

Pushed beyond endurance, Jim Gimbel lashed out. He caught his younger son a swinging blow on the side of the head, causing Davey to stagger sideways and crash into the edge of the stone stairs leading up to the old feed shed. The boy sat down, dazed.

'Davey!' shrieked his mother, flying to him. And then, to her husband, 'How could you! Raise your hand to a lad who never disobeyed you!'

Gimbel stared about him, seeing everything through a red haze of bewilderment. He swung on his heel and stumbled away, round the side of his house and through the gap in the dyke towards the open fields.

'Davey! Are you all right?' Kathy gasped, scrambling to her feet.

'Get you gone,' her mother said through her teeth. 'You've caused enough trouble for one day. Davey, lad, stand up. Come on now, come indoors and I'll put butter on that lump on your forehead ...'

'Ma, let me –'

'Go away, Kathy.' Freda turned suddenly on her daughter. 'Go away, for the love of heaven. You've brought all this on me – and I can't bear any more.'

White-faced, Kathy hurried away. When she reached the bridge she took the footpath to the riverbank and sat down on a boulder shielded by some hazel bushes just beginning to put out their catkins. There she put her face in her hands and let the tears come.

An hour later, calm again, she made her way home to Demdyke. She had to get preparations going for Joe's tea. When he came in he could sense something had upset her. He took it for granted it was the awful neighbours. He had nicknamed the two old ladies the Catty Carters but that didn't really make them funny.

'Feeling down, love?' he asked her as they sat over their cup of tea. 'Tell you what, let's go out for a drink somewhere, eh? What d'you say to a sweet sherry in the Woolpack?'

She shook her head. 'I don't think so, Joe. I always feel everybody is looking at us.'

'Oh, that's rubbish! You imagine it –'

'I don't imagine the disapproving glances I get from Amos.'

'Oh, him. Nobody pays any attention to him.'

'I'd rather not, Joe, thanks.'

'Well, let's go somewhere else, then. Shall us go to t'Feathers at Connelton? How about that! A drink in their fancy cocktail lounge.'

He was trying so hard to be good to her that she fell in with the plan. The trouble was that either because she was in an emotional state to start with or because he was too eager to enliven her, she drank too much. Too much ... she had three sweet sherries and a snowball, but then she was only accustomed to having one drink at a time.

The result was that when they got home again she was singing and giggling in a very noisy manner. No one could blame the Catty Carters nor the Powerses for looking through their curtains at them.

'Nay, now, lass, hush, hush,' Joe coaxed. 'You're making an exhibition of yourself.'

'That's right,' she carolled, 'an exhibition. Roll up, roll up, everybody, see the scarlet woman.'

'Oh, be *quiet*, Kathy!'

He ended by picking her up and carrying her indoors. Somehow he was annoyed with her. Nothing much had happened, and yet he had the feeling she had let him down.

Next day she had no memory of her own behaviour, such as it was. She had a bit of a hangover and a sense of being under a cloud, but she didn't know why. She still hadn't told Joe about the scene with her father. She had meant to, because it had been an agreement between them that they should have no secrets from each other, but somehow the moment had never seemed right yesterday. And as for today, Joe had a business appointment in Hotten, wouldn't be back at midday.

Today was a market day in Hotten. Quite a lot of men from the surrounding area would be there, seeing their bank managers and finalising business over a pint in the Lamb. Jim Gimbel went there – and his wife chose that morning for her plan.

She turned up unannounced at Demdyke. Kathy's breath was absolutely taken away when she opened the door to her.

'Ma! What are you doing here?'

'I thought I owed it to you to see you.'

'But yesterday ... yesterday you said ...'

'Aye, and I hold by that. All t'same, things are a bit altered today. I've come to say goodbye.'

'Goodbye?' Kathy echoed, her eyes wide.

Mrs Gimbel walked into the little house. To Kathy's further amazement, her brother Davey followed her in.

Davey was in his best suit. Now that Kathy looked at her mother, she realised Mrs Gimbel was in her Sunday coat.

'What's going on?' she asked as she showed them into her little living-room.

'We're leaving, Davey and me,' Freda Gimbel explained.

'But ... you can't, Ma!'

Mrs Gimbel sat down and waved Davey to do likewise. He obeyed, folding his skinny teenage length into the easy chair but looking uncomfortable.

'I've decided it's best,' Freda said. 'After yesterday, I can't take any more. I'm not well, Kathy, and I'm not going to get better living like that.'

'But you can't *leave* him! He'll be on his own!'

'Happen that's what he wants,' Freda said in a low voice. 'He hates everybody these days, even me, even his own children ... I can't go on any more, Kathy. When he hit Davey yesterday, I suddenly realised – it's no good.'

'But he was upset, Ma. He didn't really mean to hit Davey –'

'No? He did it again this morning – took the strap to him. I'm not having it, and that's the end of it.'

'But where will you go?' Kathy exclaimed. 'What'll you do?'

She couldn't imagine her mother away from Holly Farm. Freda Gimbel had been a farmer's wife for twenty-five years – what else did she know?

'I'm going to Leeds to try to get a job. There's domestic posts going, I've seen adverts for them.'

'But what about Davey?'

'I think he can get taken on as a gardener. You know he's always been good with plants. There's plenty of jobs going for housekeeper-and-gardener and things like that. There's agencies in Leeds – we'll get something.'

'But Ma –! You might hate it –'

'It can't be worse than what we've had the last twelve months,' Freda said simply. 'And if we don't like it we can always be moving on.'

'But your friends –'

'What friends?' It was a bitter reproof. 'I've never had time to make friends. I've been too hard at work on Holly Farm. The nearest thing I've got to a friend is Annie Sugden, and your father's made it impossible for me to speak to her since you moved in here.' She fetched a deep sigh. 'Nay, Kathy, I'm anxious to be gone. There's nothing here but vexation and misery.'

'But him –? What about him?'

'What about him? He won't be helped. He's closed his mind to everything.'

Davey spoke suddenly. 'I think he's ill,' he said. 'It's not just that he's bad-tempered. I think he's ill.'

'Then shouldn't you get him to see a doctor –?'

Davey shook his head. 'Don't talk daft, Kathy. When did we ever manage to get him to do anything he didn't want to?'

'I think that the shock of me going and taking Davey may make him come to his senses,' Freda said. 'I can't think of anything else that might. I'll send an address when we have one – I won't get out of touch, and if he sorts himself out and asks me to come back, I'll come and talk it over.'

'Does he know you're leaving?'

Freda almost laughed. 'Do you really think he'd let us? No, no, we're going while he's in Hotten. It's safer.'

Kathy suddenly understood that one reason impelling her mother was actual physical fear. Against that there was no argument. She might have talked on about her father's need of his wife and son, the farm work, the loneliness he would endure. But if Freda Gimbel felt he might actually strike her, or strike Davey again, there was nothing to be said

'You'll let me know where you are?' she asked.

'Aye, once we're settled. Meanwhile we'll be a night or two in a hotel or a guesthouse – I won't send you that address because we'll be gone soon from it, and anyhow I don't want anyone to know for fear it gets back to your Dad.'

'All right, Ma.' She hesitated. 'Can I get you a cup of coffee or anything?'

'No, we'd best be on our way.' Freda glanced about. 'Quite a nice little place this, after all. Happen you'll settle down here and be happy.'

'Not with old snoopy next door,' Davey said, jerking his head towards the window where the elder Miss Carter could be seen, on watch by her gate.

'At least you're not cut off from everybody,' Freda sighed. 'I feel now I didn't make enough effort to keep in touch. But it's too late now. Goodbye, Kathy.'

'Goodbye, Ma. 'Bye, Davey. You'll have to look after each other now, eh?'

Just as they were about to open the door, it opened to reveal Joe. He gaped at them. 'Mrs Gimbel! I didn't know you were coming?'

'No, neither did our Kathy. And we're just off again, Joe. We're going to Leeds.'

Joe looked from mother to son, and sensed the air of crisis. 'To Leeds? Not a holiday?'

'After yesterday, it's best to go,' Freda said with a nod at Kathy.

'Yesterday? What happened yesterday?'

'She didn't tell you?'

'Nay, what?' Joe urged. 'Somebody explain.'

'Kathy'll tell you. Davey and I have to go. I'll be in touch, Kathy.'

'Aye, and good luck, Ma.'

She went down the path with them, perhaps thinking to urge a change of mind. But no words came to her, and she had to wave them off from the gate in helpless silence.

Joe was taking off his jacket when she came in. He flung it over a chair back. 'Now, what was all this yesterday?'

'Oh ... there was a bit of a scene.'

'Where? Here?'

'Nay, up at t'farm.'

'You went up there?' he asked in horror.

'After that letter from Martin, I felt I ought to. I wanted to explain to Dad that he was driving people away. Ma said it was my fault, and I thought if I –'

'You went up there and you talked to him? After the way he ordered you out?'

'It was a big mistake. There was a terrible to-do.'

'And because of that, your mother's leaving?'

She nodded.

'As bad as that, and you never mentioned it to me?'

'I meant to, Joe. I really meant to. But we went out for the evening, and then this morning you were set on getting ready for Hotten Market.'

'You should have told me about it, Kathy. You should have told me you were going.'

'What good would that have done?'

'I'd have come with you.'

'That would only have made matters worse,' she said bluntly.

Neither of them spoke for a time. Joe had really only popped in for some papers he wanted to take up to the farm. This episode was unwanted by him, an intrusion into the time he wanted to give to financial planning – it broke up his concentration, unsteadied his thoughts. But he had to give it his attention.

He began putting his jacket on again. 'Come on,' he said, 'you'd better come up to Emmerdale.'

'What, now? What for?'

'I don't want you here on your own today – or tomorrow,

come to that. I don't want you here alone if your Dad comes rampaging in, blaming you for what's just happened. Come on, put your coat on.'

'But Joe –'

'Come *on*,' he said with impatience. Yet as he shepherded her out of the door his arm was protectively about her.

Sam Pearson made a great to-do of getting up and going out when Joe showed Kathy in. Annie Sugden witnessed it with compressed lips. 'How are you, love?' she said to Kathy, with extra warmth in her voice to try to do away with the hurt Sam had inflicted.

She bustled about, getting tea and offering biscuits. The midday meal was long over, and Joe had eaten in Hotten, but Kathy had had nothing. She wasn't hungry. She felt too dazed and bewildered to need food.

Joe got his mother alone for a moment when she went out to throw some crumbs to the birds. 'Keep her here, Ma,' he said. 'There's big trouble at Holly Farm – nowt to do wi' Kathy but I don't want her left by herself at Demdyke just for a bit.'

'She's welcome here, Joe. You know that.'

'Keep Grandad off her, eh?'

She sighed. 'I'll do my best, lad. But you know he has strong opinions.'

'Try to get him to keep 'em to himself for the time being,' Joe said, and added with a touch of humour, 'he can start being an Old Testament phrophet again tomorrow.'

Joe had to go and talk to Matt, and then there were figures to work out. Kathy didn't see much of him for the rest of that day. It made sense for them to stay to tea, at which old Sam uttered not a single word. If looks could speak, though, he said volumes. Matt and Annie kept up the conversation, chatting on with determination about the March weather, the lambs, the new feed products Joe was interested in for the cows for next autumn.

Matt walked down to Beckindale with them at the end of the day. He was concerned about them both. Kathy looked white and strained, Joe was clearly worried. When he parted from them at the far side of Mill Bridge, he was thoughtful.

'Penny for them,' Dolly said as she paused by his table with a tray of glasses.

'Eh? Was thinking about Joe, as a matter of fact ...'

'Joe? Why's he in your mind?'

'Oh well ... There's something happened up at Holly Farm. Dunno what. But it's put Joe right down in t'dumps.'

'Huh,' Dolly said with some asperity in her bright voice. 'I'd think it's done nowt to help poor Kathy either.'

Matt nodded. 'You're right. She looked right poorly.'

'Joe doesn't look after her enough,' Dolly said, picking up a dirty glass and slapping it down on her tray with some annoyance. 'He never thinks what it's like for her, cooped up there with those awful neighbours giving her the cold shoulder.'

'She been complaining?' Matt asked in surprise.

'Nay, she's not one to complain. But I've been there, I know what those old biddies are like. They're out to get her, Matt.'

He laughed. But there was no humour in Dolly's sparkling eyes. She meant it. Matt began to feel even more worried. He said defensively, 'Joe does his best. He's got a lot on his plate, you know.'

Amos moved restlessly behind the bar and, having thus attracted Dolly's attention, gave her a disapproving frown.

'Hey-up,' she sighed. 'Simon Legree doesn't like me hanging about chatting.'

As she moved away Matt said, 'You doing anything tomorrow night?'

That was her night off. She hesitated. 'Well ... I was going to see friends in Leeds.'

'Oh.'

'On the other hand, riding into Leeds on a moped in this wind isn't much fun.'

She looked at him, waiting. Come on, she was thinking, offer to drive me.

'Miss Acaster,' Amos called, 'those glasses want washing.'

There was no alternative but to go. She was annoyed with

everybody. Men! She thought. There was Joe, too insensitive to be helpful to Kathy in the midst of her troubles. There was Amos, being high-handed and demanding. And there was Matt, almost at the other extreme – too shy to ask her out when she opened the way for him.

But perhaps that was because of Lucy Stubbs. Dolly had glimpsed Lucy once or twice, and heard that Matt seemed to like her. Luckily her work seemed to keep her busy elsewhere.

What on earth did she mean, 'luckily'? Dolly shook herself and set about running hot water for her tray of washing up. It was of no interest to her one way or the other if Matt Skilbeck saw Lucy Stubbs.

The next day Dolly went to call on Kathy, but got no reply at Demdyke Row. The younger Miss Carter popped her head out of the window. 'If you're looking for that Kathy Davis,' she said, 'she's gone up to them folks at Emmerdale Farm.'

'Thank you,' Dolly said politely. 'It's nice of you to be so helpful.'

Miss Carter slammed the window down.

Dolly found Kathy working in the calf shed. 'Joe thought it were best for me to be here,' she said.

'Well, you're better off here than boxed up at Demdyke.'

'You know,' Kathy said, 'apart from the Sugden family and my Ma and brother yesterday, you're the only person in Beckindale I've had a conversation with in months.'

'It can't be as bad as that, Kathy.'

'Can't it?'

Dolly had a naturally bright, optimistic nature. She couldn't listen to Kathy's depression without wanting to help. 'Come on, love,' she said encouragingly. 'You've got Joe.'

Kathy stopped spreading the new bedding and turned to face her. 'He's cost me a lot, though, hasn't he?'

Dolly stared at her. There was something very desperate about her.

'My Dad turned his back on me, my elder brother couldn't stand the house because of the upset I'd caused and left home, when I went to try and smoothe things over there was such a row that now my Ma's left my Dad and taken Davey with her. In other words, because of me and Joe, my family's come to pieces.'

'Kathy, that's not your doing –'

'Nobody in Beckindale will talk to me –'

'Of course they will! You're imagining all the criticism –'

'You don't see it from my viewpoint. They flinch when I come up to them. Some of them cross the road to avoid me. Even here, at Emmerdale ...'

'Nobody here would say an unkind word, Kathy,' Dolly objected, thinking of Matt.

'Have you ever heard Joe's Grandad *not* saying what he thinks?' Kathy inquired with a wry smile.

Dolly thought for a moment. 'You've got Joe,' she repeated. 'Never mind all the rest – you've got someone who makes it worth while.'

'I'm not even sure of that,' Kathy said, but in a whisper so low that Dolly didn't really catch it.

For one more day Joe made sure Kathy wasn't left alone at Demdyke. He genuinely feared her father would descend on her and scare her to death. But by the end of the week he felt things had settled down enough to leave Kathy on her own. She didn't know whether to be glad or sorry. It had been nice to spend the day at Emmerdale, but there had always been the stony disapproval of Sam Pearson to face at mealtimes. To get back to the peace of Demdyke was pleasant at first, but the silence began to tell on her before midday. When she switched on her transistor for some cheerful music, someone in the Carter household banged on the wall in protest.

She picked up her coat and her handbag and hurried out. She didn't really know where she was going – all she knew was she had to get out of the house, before she made a fool of herself by screaming at the Carters.

She found Joe in the High Street, just coming out of the Post Office. The Land-Rover was by the kerb. 'Joe!' she called, over-eager. 'Fancy you being here!'

He paused, surprised at her manner. 'I'm often here,' he said, teasing. 'I live in this village.'

'Joe, are you going anywhere special?'

'I was just going into Hotten to get some stuff from the vet. Want to come?'

'Oh, I'd love to.'

She was still too fervent about it. He felt uneasy at her way of speaking. 'Anything wrong?' he asked. 'Carters been acting up?'

'Oh, not more than usual. Come on, let's go.'

'Half a mo.' He was thinking. 'Look, I'll tell you what, Kath ... If you want to get away from the house for a bit, it'd be a help if you'd go to Hotten for me.'

'You mean on my own?' Her face dropped.

'It'd be doing me a big favour. I'm needed at Emmerdale – we're sorting sheep for market.'

'But I...'

'If it's just to get out of the house? You could drive in by yourself, have a bite to eat, look at t'shops ...'

'Big deal.'

He looked hurt. 'Well, if it's no fun, why did you ask to go in the first place?'

'It's not that. I wanted ... I thought it would be nice if we went together.'

'It makes more sense if you go on your own and I get back to t'sheep.'

She knew better than to argue about that. A farmer's daughter, she understood that personal matters had to take second place. At any rate, it was better to get to Hotten than to stay cooped up at Demdyke.

'How about your dinner, then?' she asked, being practical.

'I'll get mine with Ma.'

'All right then.'

He gave her the list of things to get from the vet and the farmers' co-operative. His mind was already on the sheep Matt was sorting at Emmerdale. Kathy drove to Hotten comforting herself with the thought that she could have something exotic for lunch – a Chinese meal, or Italian, happen.

She was sitting eyeing an array of little bowls of rice, bean shoots, and noodles when a voice addressed her. It was the vicar of Beckindale.

'Mind if I join you?' he asked.

She waved him to the seat on the other side of the table. 'Feel free. I didn't know you were a fan of Chinese food.'

'I saw you through the window,' he said. 'I thought I'd take the opportunity of a word.' The waiter came up at that moment, and Hockley, after a cursory glance, ordered the Number Eight meal.

Kathy meanwhile had been studying him. 'What's up?' she asked.

'I was at Holly Farm earlier today,' he said.

Her eyes widened. 'What took you there?'

'I try to get round my flock bit by bit,' he said. 'And I'd a feeling something had happened. Your mother wasn't at church yesterday.'

'She's gone,' she said.

He drew in a breath. 'So that's it.'

'Did you see my father?'

Hockley sighed. 'I *saw* him. He wouldn't talk to me. He kept walking away from me. He was in the field next the river when I saw him, and he made off when I called, so I walked round by the road and caught him coming out the gate. But he marched on, towards the house, and all I could get out of him was that he was too busy for chat.'

'That's true enough,' she said with a frown. 'I can't imagine how he's managing.'

'Do I ... do I gather that he's on his own there now?'

'That's it.'

'Kathy, that's not right! He shouldn't be alone.'

'I know that. It's on my mind all the time.'

'Couldn't you ... go home for a bit? Help him?'

'Nay, vicar! He wouldn't let me over the threshold.'

'But ... he's your father, Kathy. You owe it to him to try.'

'No.' She was quite decisive. 'Joe would never agree to it.'

'If you explained that it was your Christian duty –?'

'Vicar,' Kathy said without bitterness, 'Joe and me have heard enough about Christianity these last months. It's not been much help to us.'

Mr Hockley said nothing. A diversion was caused by the arrival of his food. He tipped spoonfuls on to his plate and addressed himself to it, but after a mouthful or two he put his spoon down.

'I'm not saying that the church has been any help to you,' he said, 'but that doesn't mean that the principles for which it stands are wrong. Loving kindness and family affection are still valid. They ought to make you turn to your father.'

'I tried, vicar. He was in the middle of literally throwing me off his property when Davey intervened and Dad hit him.'

Mr Hockley was shocked, but recovered after a minute or two.

'Try ringing him. That at least would be something.'

'I've tried that. He either doesn't answer or he puts the phone down.'

'Since your mother left?'

'No.'

'Try again, then.'

She got up, pushing aside the food she had scarcely touched. 'I don't think I want any of this,' she said. 'Excuse me, vicar – I've got shopping to do.'

She left him among the scatter of little dishes, staring after her in consternation.

He had succeeded in making her feel guilty. She was desperate for something to take her mind off her own crimes. When she had got the items on Joe's list she walked about for a while looking at the shops, and then remembered that she could always get a free cup of coffee at the coffee bar where she used to work.

The manageress, Mrs Small, was delighted to see her. She inquired how things were going at home, listened with half an ear to her replies, and then launched into her own story –

she was always in the midst of a torrid love-life, largely imagined. The very sound of her bubbling voice cheered Kathy up, and matters were still further improved when Bim Boothroyd walked in.

He was wearing patched denims, his hair was long, and he'd grown a beard since she last saw him. But this friend of her brother Martin's was just the right antidote to her depression.

'Hello, Kath!' he cried, embracing her and giving her a smacking kiss. 'Long time no see. How's that mad brother of yours doing? Promoted to colonel yet?'

'Bim! What are *you* doing here? I heard you'd gone to Liverpool to join a group?'

'So I did, so I did,' he said. 'Wrote four songs for them then they threw me out, the ungrateful hounds. You still singing and playing the guitar?'

Kathy laughed. It was months, perhaps a year, since she'd touched her music.

She and her brother Martin had been interested in folk music, were devotees of the Spinners and the Pentangle. At one time they had even appeared in public with Bim – but her father had soon put a stop to that. Bim was trying to be a professional musician these days, although born a farmer's son like Martin.

'You still haven't said what you're doing back in the dale,' she urged.

'I'm giving a performance,' he said grandly, 'with my own group.'

'No! Honest?'

'It's true, isn't it, Mrs Small?'

'Quite true. Mr Higgins hired him and his lads to play for the week in the Upstairs Club.'

The Upstairs Club was the nearest thing Hotten had to a disco. It was the premises above the coffee-bar, and on one or two evenings of the week provided live music. Sometimes they had a guitarist who sang to his own accompaniment, sometimes they had an accordionist or a harmonica-player. Once they'd even had a harpist. But the folk groups were the most popular.

'What nights are you playing?'

'Friday and Saturday. We've a gig in Bradford tonight and tomorrow, then we're in Keighley Wednesday and Thursday. Promise you'll come and hear us.'

'Of course I will!'

'Listen,' Bim said, struck by inspiration. 'Why don't you come to Leeds? It's right-on! Good electrical equipment, good acoustics. You'd get a better idea of how we play.'

'I don't know. I'd have to ask Joe.'

'And who's Joe, when he's at home?'

'I live with him.'

Bim stroked his beard and said nothing.

'I've got to get back,' she said all of a sudden. 'I've got things he needs for the farm.'

'Listen, I mean it about tonight. Come to Leeds to hear us. Look, this is the place.' He produced a table-card and gave it to her. 'Does Joe like folk?'

'I think so. But he's busy at the moment.'

'Come on your own then.'

'Oh, I . . .'

'Look, you're a free woman, aren't you? You're not married to him.'

Kathy laughed. 'It's never as easy as that, Bim. But I'll try to come.'

When she got back to Emmerdale Joe had gone off to the Hall to talk to Tom Stubbs about a rumour concerning the disposal of the Verney land. Kathy handed over her supplies to Matt.

'Will Joe be back for tea?' she asked.

'Might be late. Stubbs said on t'phone he had folk there – sort of committee, I think, discussing what to do about amenities now Verney's sold up.'

She walked home, feeling the loneliness of the evening closing in on her. She looked for diversion in trying a new recipe, but half-past five came, six o'clock, half-past six, and still Joe didn't come home to tea. As there was no phone at Demdyke, there was no way for him to let her knew how long he'd be.

In the end she shot the ruined meal into the wastebin and set out cheese and pickle. She left a note propped against the pickle jar: 'Gone to Leeds for the evening. Cold meat in larder if you need it. Love Kathy.'

She went to Leeds by bus and train. The club where Bim's group was playing proved to be a rather lush place, and she was glad she'd put on her best dress. Bim came to talk to her and make sure she had something to eat, though the food available was only of the bar-snack variety.

The group performed well and the audience kept asking for more. Time slipped by unnoticed. To her horror, when she at last looked at her watch, it was well past eleven and she'd missed her last connection by train and bus to Beckindale.

'Never mind,' Bim soothed, 'I'll drive you back. Hang on till the performance is over.'

That moment didn't come until nearly one o'clock. Consequently it was about two in the morning when Bim dropped her in Demdyke Row, saying a whispered goodnight with a quick kiss on the top of her head.

Groggy with fatigue, she opened the door quietly and tiptoed in. The house was quiet, she could hear the clock ticking on the mantelpiece. She made for the stairs without putting on the light.

But all at once the living-room was flooded with light. Joe sat there with his hand on the switch of the table lamp.

'Where the hell have you been?' he demanded.

CHAPTER SEVEN

Next morning Prissie Carter happened to be clipping her lawn when Joe came back from milking. 'Late night last night, Mr Sugden?' she remarked.

Joe groaned inwardly. 'Not specially,' he lied.

'We heard you. Two o'clock, it was.'

He didn't doubt she'd heard them. They had been practically shouting at each other. He was ashamed now of how angry he'd been at Kathy's outing. But her words still hurt, the words she had said in answer to his reproach: 'It's not as if we're married, after all, Joe.'

'No, but we will be,' he'd insisted. And she hadn't replied. Instead she'd gone upstairs to bed.

He hadn't seen her as yet this morning. She'd not got up when he rose for milking, and he hadn't disturbed her. But she was busy now in the kitchen; he could smell the toast and bacon from the gate.

'That would be a relative that drove up in the van last night?' Miss Carter was saying.

'A relative? Er ... no, it was a friend of Kathy's.'

'I only wondered,' Miss Carter said, 'because I saw him kiss her goodnight.'

Joe bit his lip. 'Did you have to get out of bed or could you watch without getting up?' he demanded, and strode on.

'Well, really!' said Miss Carter.

Kathy, overcome by remorse for yesterday's events, had prepared a fine breakfast – bacon, fried potatoes, mushrooms, eggs, and a pile of toast dripping with butter. Joe washed his hands without speaking and sat down. Kathy, who had turned with a smile as he came through from the living-room, eyed him with anxiety.

'You're not still annoyed about last night, are you?' she said. 'I only spent the evening with an old friend.'

'Close enough friend to kiss you goodnight?'

She gasped. 'So that's it,' she said. 'Which of them has been at you? Effie or Prissie?'

'What's it matter? If you –'

'You're right, what's it matter! You believe them without troubling to remember it's just malice on their part.'

'It isn't true then? They're telling lies?'

'No, they're speaking the truth, in their way. Bim did kiss me goodnight.'

'I see. What else happened?'

'He drove away again. You must have heard him drive up and drive away – you were waiting to pounce when I came in.'

'To pounce? For God's sake, Kathy, I'd been waiting up for you since bedtime, imagining you'd had an accident! Then you come tiptoeing in, looking on top of the world –'

'And that's all wrong, isn't it? I'm not to enjoy myself.'

'That's rubbish, Kath. You're entitled to have fun just like anybody else, but I think you ought to have let me know –'

'Did you let me know you'd not be in for tea?'

'How could I? I was shut up in a meeting at the Hall –'

'And how could I let you know I'd be late home? There's no phone here, as you must have noticed.'

'Oh, for Pete's sake!' He broke off. His raised voice was sure to penetrate to the Carters, and he didn't want to give them the satisfaction of knowing they'd caused another quarrel.

He'd sat down at the breakfast table but Kathy had so far not taken the food out of the oven. She opened the oven door and gestured to it. 'Do you want any of this?'

He got up. 'No thanks. I reckon I'll go up to Emmerdale and eat there.'

'That'll be the second meal I've cooked within twelve hours that you haven't bothered with.'

'Listen, Kathy –'

'It's a great outlook, isn't it?' she persisted, her voice cracking. 'I moved in here with you to share your life, and now I can't even cook so that you'll sit down to eat with me.'

'Oh, you know that's not it –'

'What's the point of all this, Joe? What are we doing? Kidding ourselves?'

Defeated, he went back through the living-room, picking up his jacket as he went. 'I dunno, Kathy,' he said. 'I just don't understand what's happening to us.'

When he reached the front door she called, 'Will you be back for your dinner?'

'I don't think so. I've got to go to Connelton.'

'I see.'

He turned back. 'Listen, Kathy, let's go out somewhere this evening. Let's have a meal out – Harrogate or somewhere.'

She hesitated. 'At the moment I don't feel –'

'Think about it. I'll drop by later in the day. If you want to do it, I'll ring up and book a table. What d'you say, Kath?'

'We'll see,' she said.

When he reappeared at Emmerdale, his mother set about providing his breakfast without questioning him. But his grandfather couldn't let well alone. 'Not up yet, is she? One thing a farmer needs, it's a good breakfast under his belt –'

'Dad,' Annie said warningly.

'I'm only saying – staying up late at night, coming to work with shadows under your eyes and nothing in your belly – it's no way to go on.'

'What happened at the meeting yesterday?' Annie asked, hoping to divert the conversation.

'Looks like the educational college isn't going to take up all the land available. R.S.P.B. chap was saying we ought to leave t'woodland undisturbed – there's goldcrests trying to nest there.'

'Nonsense,' Sam cried. 'I used to walk through Verney's woods every day when I was young and never saw a goldcrest.'

'What I'm saying.' Joe's voice was patient. 'They're trying to nest. One cold winter'll wipe them out though.'

'Nice little things. I've only ever seen one once,' Annie said. 'What's happening about putting in tennis courts and so forth for the college?'

'They've got planning permission for all that. County

Council chap said the college authorities might make 'em available to the local inhabitants. They may even have a lecture hall that could be used as a theatre – so we might be able to use that too. For shows and things.'

'Beckindale village hall is all right for shows,' Sam grumbled. 'When I were a lad, we didn't even have that.'

'But it's nice to have a bit of something going on,' Joe said. 'Not have to go far off in the evening –'

'If a man has a sensible wife he doesn't want to go gadding,' Sam said. 'He's happy to settle down of an evening by his fireside.'

His grandson got up, pushed his chair into its place by the table, and made for the door.

'Nay, lad, you've eaten nothing,' Annie cried.

'I'm not hungry, Ma.'

When the door had closed on him, Annie turned in sadness to her father. 'What are you trying to do?' she asked. 'Drive him away?'

'What's the matter? I only said a man ought to sit at home with his wife.'

'You were saying more than that, and we both know it.'

Sam too got up, picked up his cap, and crammed it on his head. 'I'll be in my workshop if I'm wanted,' he said, 'which doesn't seem likely as no one takes any notice of what *I* say.'

This disastrous twenty-four hours had still not spilled out all its troubles on Joe. He went to Connelton with Henry to talk to a friend and then go on to look at a trout farm in which Henry was interested. Henry had remarked that the balance of money from the sale of Hawthorn might be invested in some such scheme, but when Joe had walked round the fish farm and thought it over, he shook his head at it.

'Well, I'm not saying this is the investment,' Henry said. 'But we ought to do something with that money.'

Joe had repaid all he had borrowed plus the interest. The trailer had been bought. There was still a substantial remainder.

'It's on deposit,' Joe said. 'It's earning interest.'

'Minimum lending rate. That's nowt. We ought to do better than that. Have you thought of trying for any of the Verney land?'

'I've thought of it. Decided against it.'

'Oh? You didn't mention it to me.'

'Well, since I'd decided against it, there didn't seem much point, did there, Henry?'

'I've heard that's excellent land. We could go into arable –'

'I don't think so.'

'Why not? There's money in it –'

'Not on the scale we'd be doing it. Besides, we could only buy a few acres at current prices for the money we've got.'

'We could talk to the bank –'

'We're discussing what to do with the balance from Hawthorn, not going in for big-scale investment.'

'Well, the way I see it, we're only standing still since we got the attestation.'

'That's not right. We're improving the sheep all t'time, and we're moving into beef. That's enough for t'present.'

'Well, it's a bit stick-in-the-mud –'

'Henry,' Joe said, suddenly tired of the argument, 'I've enough on my plate at the moment without having to think what to do with that money. When I've got time, I'll get round to it.'

'Hm.' Henry tugged at his moustache. 'A businessman shouldn't allow personal matters to interfere with the way he conducts his business.'

'On the other hand,' Joe replied, 'he shouldn't rush into things when he knows he's not making good judgements.'

'Regretting things, are you?'

Joe frowned at him, and pointed to the piping that kept the water running fresh and strong through the farm. 'We might find out how much that kind of piping costs,' he said. 'We could do with something like that to take water out to stock, happen.'

Henry, thus rebuked for his tactless remark, coloured and let the conversation take a new turn. But Joe felt the question rankling all through the drive back to Beckindale.

He said goodbye to Henry and drove on to Demdyke. As he put on the handbrake Mrs Bamforth, from Number Seven, bounced out waving at him. 'Mr Sugden, Mr Sugden!'

'What now?' he groaned just below his breath. He got out. She hustled up to him, holding down her print apron against the sharp wind.

'*Mr Sugden*!' she began importantly. 'I think you should speak to them Carters! It's too much, really it is!'

'Speak to the Carters? They won't speak to *me*.'

'Nay, I don't mean that. I mean, complaining to the Council –'

'Who? Me?'

'No no, *them*!'

'They've complained?' Joe said, mystified. It hardly seemed likely that even the Carters would carry a complaint to the Council about a couple living outside the bonds of wedlock.

The story, when he had sifted it from Mrs Bamforth's exclamatory style, was tragi-comic. Someone – and Mrs Bamforth was sure it was the Carters – had complained that mice were infesting the houses in Demdyke Row from Joe's house. The rodent-operative – or ratcatcher, as he used to be known before gobbledegook took over – had spent the morning turning the house upside down while Kathy watched in dismay. Finding no mice, the rodent-operative had then gone from house to house.

'Fair spoiled my baking,' Mrs Bamforth wailed. 'Draughts as he walked in and out – my sponge cake's like leather.'

'But if he found the mice –'

'There aren't any mice! Never have been! It's sheer nastiness, that's what it is.'

Joe went indoors, calling Kathy's name. But she wasn't there. Kathy had in fact gone off on her bike to Hotten to speak to the Health Officer at the Council offices. But in her anger and dismay she'd quite forgotten that Joe had said he'd be back to see her soon after lunch. He hung about, but in the end had to get back to Emmerdale. He was beginning to feel they were destined not to come together in the same room these days.

As he worked with Matt through milking, Joe was quiet. Matt said: 'What did you think to t'fish farm?'

'Not for us. Money in it, I don't doubt – but it's too specialised.'

'What did Henry say?'

'Not much ... Matt, are you doing anything this evening?'

'Well ... I was going to go down to Woolpack, have a chat with Dolly.'

'Thought you were taking Lucy Stubbs out?'

'That's tomorrow.'

'One round of giddy pleasure,' said Joe. 'I were going to ask – how'd you like to come out with Kathy and me? Make a foursome?'

'Tomorrow?'

'Well, I was going to suggest tonight, but if your date with Lucy's tomorrow, happen it'd be best to arrange it for then. What d'you say?'

'I'd have to ring Lucy and find out.'

'Will you do that, then? I'd like to take Kathy out. Sort of brighten things up.'

'Better if it were just the pair of you, surely.'

Joe shook his head. 'No-o ... We'd be better with some company. Less likely to get into an argument.'

'Joe ...'

'What?'

'I were just going to say, if you have to have other folk there so as not to argue ... summat's wrong.'

'Aye,' Joe sighed. 'You could say that.'

The idea of the evening out together came to nothing. Joe got home to Demdyke for tea, to find Kathy keyed up and dressed for diversion. She had had a rotten day, ending with a passage of arms at the Council offices and a puncture on the ride home. She wanted more than anything in the world to go out and be in some pleasant place where she could forget it all.

'Nay, love, I've put it off till tomorrow,' Joe said. 'I invited Matt to come too, and bring Lucy –'

'You what?'

'I thought it would be more fun for you – have someone to talk to – another girl –'

'You changed it without telling me?'

'But you weren't here when I came in, Kathy.'

'No, I was in Hotten having a fight about that rotten pair next door and their lies! And now you tell me we're not going out!'

'We can go out if you want to – down the Woolpack –'

'But you said we'd go to Harrogate!'

'I never booked the table, Kathy –'

'But I've been looking forward to it all day.'

'Well, look, let's have us teas and then we'll go somewhere for a drink – Connelton or Littlewell –'

'Tea? But I haven't cooked anything. I thought you were taking me out.'

'Oh, heck! We can rake something up out of the larder –'

'But I want to go *out*!'

'Listen, Kathy, I've had a rotten day, let's sit down over a cup of tea and something to eat –'

Driven beyond endurance, Kathy walked straight past him and out through the door.

She didn't come home till after midnight. Though Joe hadn't stayed up, he was still awake. And the sound of the car engine told him it was the same van that had brought her home on Monday.

From the events of those few days they never really recovered. Even the fact that Beckindale was planning a great many social activities didn't seem to involve them. The rest of the village was seething with enthusiasm; it seemed to sweep past Joe and Kathy, like a tide leaving driftwood on the shore.

Beckindale was engaged in trying to raise enough money to put a new heating system into the parish church. An elderly couple called Baxter had left a sum of money for a stained glass window which Mr Hockley thought would be better used for the heating. Annie had resisted this and had carried the day when the matter was referred to the bishop. Now Mr Hockley was trying to raise the money for the heating system by other means, chief of which was a village concert.

To everyone's delight, Dolly Acaster proved a great asset. It turned out she had hidden abilities as a scene painter – it appeared she had worked with an amateur theatrical company in Leeds.

Dolly suddenly became one of the most important young ladies in Beckindale. She was quite unaccustomed to so much approval, for her employer Mr Brearley was one of those who believed that if you handed down too much praise, it gave your employees ideas above their station.

To be given complete control of the sets and decorations for the concert was a great compliment. She knew she had talent, and after much sketching in the privacy of her digs at night, came out with a beautiful colour scheme depending on swathes of cloth cleverly folded and draped.

'Looks a bit odd, doesn't it?' Mr Hockley said when he inspected it at the halfway stage. 'Still, I know she's got it all planned.'

'Oh, yes, she's a grand lass,' Henry Wilks said with pride. He still thought he'd been very shrewd to get her to work in the Woolpack. Even since she arrived, they'd had increased profits. Moreover, she could cook, and when Amos would let her she did, producing tasty little snacks from the small oven in the kitchen.

Dolly wanted very much to better herself in the job she'd chosen. Her ambition was to run a pub of her own one day. But in the months since she came to the Woolpack she felt she'd been marking time. She'd learned something about cellaring from Amos, but he never let her use her talents properly.

So when Henry's friend George Bailey rang her to offer her a job in his brewery chain, she was greatly tempted.

George Bailey was the man who had first brought her to

Henry's notice. He had no compunction about making an offer for her services, even though he knew full well she was in the midst of producing the backcloth for the village concert.

'After all, Miss Acaster, you're in business to make a career, not to help out with amateur theatricals.'

'That's true, Mr Bailey, but I'd feel bad about letting them down.' And besides, there was Matt Skilbeck. Not that he had anything to do with it, really. All the same, she recalled the little surge of delight she felt when she heard his date with Lucy Stubbs had fallen through. She didn't know the ins and outs of it, but it seemed that Joe and Matt were going to go out in a foursome with Kathy and Lucy. But Kathy had turned against the idea after it was all arranged, and then when Matt rang Lucy to re-arrange it all again, she'd gone in the huff.

But that ought not to influence her decision about this new job. No, nor would it. She'd think it through with no bias one way or the other. She really would rather stay on in Beckindale until after the concert, because of painting their scenery for them – but Mr Bailey wanted her to start almost at once in Ingleton . . . Goodness, wasn't life complicated!

She was hurrying up and down ladders in the village hall when Matt came to offer his help. She was annoyed with herself for brightening so visibly when he came in. But then, that was because he was taller than she was and far more accustomed to standing on ladders. She handed bunting up to him, and he pinned it in place according to her instructions.

' 'Bye, you've an eye for all this,' he said in admiration. 'I'd no idea it could look like this in here! I thought it needed repainting.'

'Well, it does. But since there's no money for that, the next best thing is camouflage.'

'But how d'you know the colours are going to go with everything? I'd have thought blue and green together would look too dark.'

'Nay, you have to choose the right shades, that's all. And a touch of magenta here and there just brings out the tones.'

'Hand me up that long bit.'

They tangled themselves in a long strip of blue cotton. Matt couldn't help thinking that she looked extremely pretty, all flushed from the exertion. And when she smiled at him in gratitude for his help, he felt warm inside.

'What about the bits round the lights?'

'Can't stop to do that,' she sighed. 'I've got to get back to the Woolpack. I'm late already.'

She was indeed. Amos Brearley, beset by an influx of customers from a car rally that evening, was almost beside himself.

'Condescended to come back, have you?' he said between his teeth as she came in.

'I'm sorry,' she said at once. 'I got interested in t'decorations at t'hall –'

'You're paid to work here, not in t'hall!'

'I know that, Mr Brearley, but –'

'Of course you're lapping it up, aren't you? The limelight, I mean.'

'Nowt o't'sort –'

'There's a customer there wants serving!'

'Yes – sorry –'

She hurried to the other end of the bar and got to work. In the course of coping with the gins and vodkas ordered by the car rally group, she got in a momentary muddle.

'Pay attention,' Amos hissed. 'This is important, not like your daft goings on in the village hall.'

'I'm doing my best, Mr Brearley –'

'It's a poor best, isn't it?'

To do Amos justice, he was in a bad temper because he himself had had a hard day. But he had no idea how wrongly he was affecting Dolly. She had almost decided to say no to the job from Mr Bailey until this moment – perhaps because of having spent a pleasant half-hour with Matt Skilbeck. Now her hackles were raised.

'Mr Brearley,' she said, turning to him and leaving her

customers with their tongues hanging out, 'are you saying I'm bad at my job?'

'All you know you learned here by picking my brains,' said Amos wrathfully.

'Right.' To his astonishment she walked away from the bar, through the doorway to the back kitchen.

Tongue-tied, Amos watched her go. She went through the kitchen, by the passage to the front of the pub, and there put some money in the coinbox of the public telephone. When Amos caught up with her, she was replacing the receiver.

'Here!' he began.

But she brushed past him. When he caught up with her again she was collecting her crash helmet from the back room.

'Where are you going?' he gasped.

'Home.'

'But you can't – you can't go – you're on duty in the bar!'

'No I'm not.'

'But you are! This evening is your night on –'

'Oh yes, after weeks of slaving in the kitchen doing the washing-up, and carting boxes of mixers about, you actually let me work in the bar last week and this week – and tonight because I'm a few minutes late coming on, you bite my head off.'

'You listen to me, Dolly Acaster –'

'I've listened to you long enough, Mr Brearley.'

She walked on, and he padded along behind her. She came through the saloon bar. Conversation stopped as she appeared. Annie Sugden, who had dropped in with Matt for a drink after a stint at the village hall, looked at her angry face with dismay.

'What's happening?' she asked, half-rising from her chair.

'I'm leaving, Mrs Sugden. I'm leaving Beckindale.'

'What – you mean for good?'

'For good. I've been offered a pub down Ingleton way – Mr Bailey rang me at the beginning of the week.'

'But you can't go, Dolly!' Annie cried. 'What about the backcloth?'

'You'll have to get someone else to finish it.'

'But no one else knows how!'

'I'm sorry, Mrs Sugden. You'll just have to do the best you can.'

Matt had been dumbfounded by the turn of events. He found his voice. 'Couldn't you ... couldn't you just stay till after the concert, Dolly?'

If anyone could have persuaded her, it was Matt. But she had made her decision. 'No, I'm sorry. Happen I'll see you at my new place – you know where it is, just south of Ingleton.'

'Miss Acaster!' cried Amos, after a glance around at the throng of customers. 'You can't walk out on me like this! Where's your sense of loyalty?'

'Where's your sense of appreciation?' she flashed back. 'I was willing and eager to do everything I could to make things a success here, but you've never said a kind word to me since I arrived.'

'Kind words isn't the way to train a hotelier,' Amos said, calling on his dignity.

'And unkind words aren't the way to earn loyalty,' riposted Dolly.

Leaving them speechless, she walked out.

This public drama was a talking point in the village next day. A more private drama was unnoticed.

For some days Annie had felt that her son was under a great strain. It seemed to date from the evening when – as she understood it – he and Kathy were to have gone out in a foursome with Matt and Lucy. She herself happened upon Kathy in Hotten some days later, which after all was a very small town – and Kathy had turned and hurried away.

Troubled, Annie went to the coffee bar where Kathy used to work. She knew Kathy still went there sometimes to keep up with old acquaintances. Outside the door, a battered old Dormobile was parked, and a young man in faded jeans, a T-shirt labelled 'Penitentiary of San Quentin', and safari boots was loading musical instruments in the back.

The important thing to Annie was that Kathy was helping him.

For one terrible moment Annie thought the girl was packing to leave. But they kissed goodbye, and the man got into the driving seat and drove off.

Annie joined Kathy as she went into the coffee bar. 'Friend of yours?' she asked.

'A friend of Martin's. He just stopped off to collect some stuff he left.'

'How are you, Kathy? You haven't been up to the farm in nearly a month.'

'I've been busy.'

'I see.' Annie hesitated. 'You hurried off when I saw you earlier.'

'I wanted to get there in time to say goodbye to Bim.' Kathy sighed. 'In fact, I think I was intending to be in time to go with him.'

'Kathy!'

'Oh, don't worry, it was only a passing thought.'

Annie took her by the elbow. 'Come inside, I'll buy you a cup of coffee.'

'Nay, Mrs Small will give us a cup for free.' They went in and found themselves a quiet spot behind a potted palm.

'The divorces become absolute in a few weeks, don't they?' Annie said as she stirred the foam on her capucino.

'Yes.'

'You and Joe are getting married straight away?'

The girl made no reply. When Annie looked up, their eyes met. There were tears somewhere in the depths of Kathy's.

'Ah, lass, how have things gone so wrong?' Annie asked.

'I don't know, Mrs Sugden. I really don't. It's nothing either of us has done. Nothing serious, I mean.'

'But you're still fond of each other, surely?'

'Aye, fond as ever – when we're not having a row.'

'Is there anything I can do?'

'I don't think there's anything *anybody* can do.'

They sipped their coffee. Annie said, 'How're you getting back? Do you want a lift?'

'I'll go back by bus.'

'But there isn't a bus now until eight o'clock!'

'I'm staying until eight o'clock.'

'But ...'

'But what's Joe going to do about his tea? Same as he's done other evenings – manage on his own.'

'Kathy, this is no way to go on ...'

'It's best, Mrs Sugden. We only argue when we're together.'

There was little that could be said in the face of such pessimism. Annie could only hope that time would improve matters. Perhaps when the divorces came through and the suspense was over, everything could go back to normal.

But now she knew why Joe had seemed so strained recently.

Joe wasn't surprised to find Kathy gone out when he got back to Demdyke that evening. Over the past few weeks it had become quite usual. He couldn't blame her. There seemed nowhere that she could go and be at home. Her own house was made unbearable by the illwill of the Carters, Emmerdale was uncomfortable because of his grandfather's disapproval, Holly Farm was barred to her by her own father's rejection. Beckindale itself had little to offer. It wasn't strange that she'd taken to spending her afternoon and evening in Hotten, where there were one or two acquaintances with whom she could pass the time.

Yet sometimes when she came back, emotion would sweep them both. There would be a passionate reconciliation. He would think that everything was going to be all right – only to wake up next morning to life with a stranger.

How was it he had known so little about Kathy when they first came to live here? He had known her all his life, had been in love with her for months – and he had utterly failed to understand her in the last few weeks. Her moods baffled him. Her sense of guilt perplexed him. He knew she blamed herself for the way her family had broken apart, but he was sure she was over-reacting. Her father was the main culprit, but she would never allow him to say that now.

When she came in about nine o'clock, he was watching television. He switched it off, hoping to have a conversation. She went into the kitchen. He got up and went after her.

'All right, love?'

She shrugged. 'I saw your mother in Hotten today,' she said.

'Oh?'

'I think she's worried about you.'

'Nay, she sees me every day. She knows there's nowt wrong wi' me.'

'Joe,' she cried, turning away from the dresser and letting fall the cup she'd been holding, 'what are we doing to each other?'

'Now, lass – nay, don't take on . . .'

She stooped to pick up the cup. 'It's broken,' she said dully.

'We'll buy another.'

'Aye,' she said. 'If it was only as easy as that.'

They made some tea and sat together in the living-room, but they were miles apart. She went to bed about ten and he, weary beyond words at the gulf that had opened between them, dozed all night in the armchair.

He went out as usual at five-thirty to milk at Emmerdale. When he came back for breakfast, Kathy was nowhere to be found. He made a mountain of toast and wolfed it down. Once his hunger was assuaged he had a look to see what Kathy's plans might have been. Her bike was gone, which seemed to mean she'd decided to cycle into Hotten or Littlewell.

He left a note for her: 'See you dinnertime.'

He was driving back to Emmerdale when Barney the postman flagged him down. 'Give's a lift to the phone, Joe,' he said.

'Your post office bike gone wrong, then?'

'Nay, it's no laughing matter. I've been up to Holly Farm to deliver a registered letter – can't get a reply.'

'What? But – there must be someone there. Did you look in t'barns?'

'Aye, and I'll tell thee what,' Barney said, his narrow face creased in anxiety. 'Cows were lowing in pain – they've not been milked.'

'You what?' It was unheard-of. No farmer would neglect his livestock.

'Come on, turn around, Joe. I want to get to phone-box. I'm calling t'police.'

CHAPTER EIGHT

Joe dropped Barney at the phone box then swept round in a racing curve that caused windows to be opened in Beckindale. He drove back the way he'd come but instead of turning for Emmerdale he made for the Beckin Bridge and the road to Holly Farm. He could hear the cows as he got out of the Land-Rover. He hurried to the cowshed and there they were, pressing into the stalls, heads moving restlessly, voices raised, udders full. Without stopping to think about it he set to, attaching the old-fashioned machinery that Gimbel had never been able to replace, soothing the confused creatures whose world had been turned topsy-turvy.

He was still at work when he heard the police car roll into the yard. He ran out. A constable came up to him. 'You belong here?'

'Nay, Joe Sugden, from next door farm. The postman told me there'd been nothing done to the milkers – I'm seeing to it.'

'Been in the house?'

'No.'

'Would you come along with us, sir? You know the place, I presume?'

'Should do. He's been our neighbour as long as I can remember.'

The house door was locked. So was the back door. They looked through the windows but nothing could be seen except the remains of a meal on the kitchen table and some neglected plants in the parlour.

'Would you say he's in there somewhere? Ill, perhaps?'

Joe blew out a breath. 'Constable, there's summat wrong.

He'd never leave his animals like that.'

'I think we'll have to break in.' The constable frowned. 'I'll just call in and report what I'm doing.'

'Aye. I'd better get back to t'mistle.'

He finished up in the cowshed. When he had done that and fed the hens, he heard another vehicle coming up the lane. He dashed out. An ambulance was lurching over the uneven surface.

Joe ran after it. When he reached the house door, the constable came out, putting out an arm to stop him. He motioned the ambulance men to go in.

'You found him, then?'

The policeman nodded.

'Heart attack?'

'No. Gunshot wounds.'

'What?'

'He's bad. You know him well, I take it. Any reason for his wanting to do a thing like that?'

'You mean he – he – ?'

'I'm afraid so, sir. What about his family? Has he a wife?'

'Aye. And three children – a daughter and two sons.'

'But there's nobody here, Mr – Sugden, is it?'

Joe bent his head. 'Nobody here,' he repeated in a whisper.

A moment later the ambulance men came out carrying a stretcher bearing a blanketed figure. They went quickly past, loaded the stretcher into the ambulance, and were off with the siren going. The constable went to his car to report his actions. Joe stood as if turned to stone.

How was he going to tell this to Kathy?

After a moment or two the policeman came back to him. 'Can you tell me how to get in touch with the family you mentioned? His wife?'

Joe shook his head. 'She ... she left. Couple of months ago.'

'Ah.' A pause. 'The others then? The sons?'

'One of them is with his Ma. The other went in t'Army. The daughter is ... living in Beckindale. Kathy Davis.'

'Oh, married daughter? I see. Her address is –?'

'She lives in Demdyke Row, that turning off behind t'old mill. But she's not there.'

'Out at work?'

'No. But she's gone out.'

The constable, an experienced man, studied Joe. There was more to this than met the eye. 'You know the family well, sir?'

'I've told you – we've been neighbours all us lives. Kathy and me ... she's getting a divorce ... it's understood ...'

'I see, sir. You say she's gone out – do you know where?'

'No idea. She took her bike – might have gone to Hotten or Littlewell, even to Loudwick.'

'Market day at Loudwick,' the constable mused. 'She might have gone there for the shopping.' He made a move towards his car then paused. 'You don't have an address for Mrs Gimbel?'

'No, but Kathy has it.'

'It's clear she's the first person to get in touch with.' He went away and talked earnestly into his r/t set for some minutes. When he had done all he could there, he leaned out to call to Joe. 'Who should we contact meanwhile, Mr Sugden? Anyone in the village who would have any idea of what brought him to this state?'

'I dunno ... The vicar?'

'Can you accompany us there, then? I'd best let him know what's happened, see if he can tell us anything.'

Joe hesitated. 'I ought to hang on here. There's things need doing.'

'Couldn't we get someone else to stand in?'

Joe made up his mind. 'I'll sort it – ring from t'Woolpack. Come on then.'

The thought of taking action helped to steady him. He led the police car to the vicarage, then drove to the Woolpack and rang his mother. Annie was aghast at his news.

'How is he, Joe?'

'Dunno. They rushed him to hospital. Thing is, Ma – I'm worried about the livestock and that ...'

'I'll get Matt. Leave it with me, Joe. And Joe –'

'Yes?'

'How's Kathy taking it?'

'She don't know, Ma. I don't know where she is.'

The rest of the morning passed in a flurry of useless activity, as far as Joe was concerned. He rang round everywhere he could think of in search of Kathy, but without success. He couldn't help feeling it was like that nightmare night when Matt's children had died – they'd spent hours then, trying to find Matt. One of those repeating nightmares, that you couldn't escape from.

The vicar proved a tower of strength. He went at once with the police to the hospital, and from there reported back from time to time. It was he who spotted Kathy, as the police car brought him home from the hospital. She was cycling past on her way to Beckindale. At a word from Hockley the driver touched the hee-haw and then signalled her to stop.

Kathy came to a stumbling halt. Hockley got out of the car in a scramble. 'Where have you been, Kathy? We've been looking for you since eight o'clock.'

'Why? What's up?' Her first thought was an accident to Joe. She went white.

'It's your father. I'm afraid he's in a bad way.'

'Dad? What happened?'

'Look, leave your bike on the verge and come with us.'

'Where to? Is he at home –?'

'He's in hospital. Don't waste time, Kathy – I'll explain as we go.'

But though the driver made it as fast as he could, they were too late. Jim Gimbel died while Kathy was on her way.

Joe had gone back to Emmerdale by that time. There were things he had to see to, and he wanted to speak to his mother about the event. She asked at once if he had had dinner.

'I couldn't eat, Ma, thanks.'

'Sit you down. Have a cup of tea, at least. What exactly happened, Joe?'

'He tried to do himself in. With a shotgun.'

Annie said nothing for a moment. To her, to take one's own

life was a sin. Life belonged to God – man hadn't the right to say when it should end. But she could pity from her heart the misery and exhaustion of the spirit that had driven Jim Gimbel to do this dreadful act.

'Have you got in touch with Kathy yet?'

'Not yet.'

'Drink the tea, Joe. It helps nothing if you get worn out.'

'Matt's up at Holly Farm, is he?'

'Aye, and Grandad went too. He felt . . . he felt he owed it to Jim.'

'Aye, we all feel guilty now, I s'pose,' Then quickly, 'Not you, Ma. You did your best.'

'Don't exonerate me,' she sighed. 'I didn't try hard enough.'

Joe glanced at his watch. 'Who's going to do milking here?'

'You and I'll have to do it. Matt and Grandad will stay up at Holly Farm.'

'Right.' He drank up his tea. 'I've got to find Kathy. I'll go back to Demdyke – happen she's home again by now. I'll be here in time for milking.'

His mother nodded agreement and watched him hurry away with an aching heart. She had said little because that was her way, but she longed to be able to do something to help. She had a feeling that today's events would prove crucial to his relationship with Kathy.

When he drove up to Demdyke Row the vicar was just coming out of the house. Joe jumped out of the Land-Rover – it must mean Kathy was home.

To his surprise the vicar blocked his way. 'Don't go in, Joe.'

'But I –'

'She's very upset. I ought to warn you, she needs a minute to get over it.'

'How did you find her?'

'Cycling back from Connelton.'

'Connelton? What the dickens was she doing there?' Then, with a gesture that said, What does that matter, he added quickly, 'I've got to talk to her.'

'Joe . . .'

'Well?'

'She's packing to go home.'

That was the end of the conversation. Joe pushed past and went into his house.

But he hadn't allowed time for the vicar to give him one important piece of news.

When he got indoors, Kathy was just coming downstairs with a carrier bag in her hands, from which the handle of her hairbrush stuck out.

'Kathy!' he burst out. 'Look, don't go like this –'

She reached the foot of the stairs and passed him into the living-room. 'I'm going, Joe.'

'But what's the point? He's in hospital – and if they let him home he –'

His words died away at the expression on her face.

'What's up?' he said, stricken.

'He's dead, Joe.'

There was nothing to say to that. He sat down on the nearest chair.

'He died before I could get to t'hospital. I didn't even get a chance to tell him . . . tell him . . .'

'Kathy! Nay, lass, don't –'

'If I hadn't left home, he'd probably still be alive now. It's my fault he did what he did.'

'That's rubbish! You didn't want to go – he drove you out! When you tried to make it up wi' him, he *threw* you out!'

'I'm not defending him, Joe. But he had his views, and he lived up to them. I ought to have respected him more.'

'Respect a man who drove away his entire family? Martin into t'Army, your Ma and Davey –'

'And lived on there alone. I should have realised how awful it was for him.'

'It's not going to help if you go and do t'same –'

'I've got to live somewhere, haven't I?'

Joe got to his feet, came to stare down at her. 'What's wrong with here?' he asked quietly.

She met his eyes, and for a long moment they gazed at each other. Then she said, with suppressed bitterness: 'It was bad enough before. They were out to make me seem a wicked woman. Now they've really got something to get their teeth in, haven't they? Drove my Dad to suicide!'

'But that's not true! And anyhow, since when did we live our lives to suit what other folks think?'

'Oh yes!' She turned away, her movement almost irritable. 'It doesn't matter, does it? That's why we've been living this dream existence –'

'But you take it so much to heart, Kathy –'

'So would you, if you had my conscience.'

'You've nothing to reproach yourself with. You –'

'I don't have to reproach myself. Other folk do it for me! I can't go on like that. I can't go on living here.'

'But, for heaven's sake, Kath! That doesn't mean you have to go to Holly Farm –'

'It does.' She put a lipstick from the mantelpiece into her carrier. 'I'm Jim Gimbel's daughter, the only member of the family available to do anything with the responsibilities he left. Until I can make other arrangements, I'm going to live in my father's house.'

Her tone was cold, almost hard. He studied her, and knew it was useless to try to persuade her otherwise, for the moment at least. 'I'll give you a lift there with your things,' he offered in a voice he kept very calm.

'I can manage on my own, Joe,' she said.

The total rejection in the words told him there was nothing to be done. He shook his head at her in helpless acceptance, then went out. When he got into the Land-Rover he had an impulse to go back, to try again. But a police car came into the lane and he realised this was to be her transport to Holly Farm.

And the neighbours came out to see what was going on. So he drove away.

The week that followed seemed to go on for ever. An inquest was held; verdict, death by gunshot wounds, self-inflicted while the balance of his mind was disturbed. Joe attended but he wasn't called to give evidence – the presence of the police constable at the scene had made other evidence almost superfluous. Constable Kemp told tersely what he had done and the medical evidence was the only other material. As they left the court, Joe watched to see if Kathy would turn to him, but she kept out of his way.

Next came the news of what was to happen to Holly Farm. It was a rented farm; the lease was bought by a farmer from Ribblesdale, who was prepared to take over the stock and equipment at a low price.

'Not worth more, is it?' Henry Wilks said in a bluff, practical tone when he heard.

'Doesn't leave much to Mrs Gimbel, though, does it?'

'She coming to the funeral?'

'I reckon.'

'You going, Joe?'

'Of course he's going,' Annie said. 'We're neighbours. Whole family will go.'

Henry looked around the comfortable kitchen at Emmerdale. 'Neighbours,' he sighed. 'But couldn't be more different ...'

The funeral was formal, dignified. Only family and neighbours were present. Beckindale felt it ought not to attend the funeral of a man who had taken his own life, although there were those who would dearly have liked to know what the Reverend William Hockley would say in his funeral address.

Hockley was perturbed about it himself. He was a tolerant man, but he felt he couldn't condone what Gimbel had done. God called upon man to bear his burdens, not to evade them. But in the end his kind heart told him to speak gently. He quoted the passage from St Matthew: 'Strait is the gate, and narrow is the way which leadeth unto life, and few there be that find it.' He suggested that Jim Gimbel had been one of those who for all his searching had never quite found the path 'which leadeth unto life', and had needed more love and understanding than perhaps anyone could give. 'We ought all to learn from this, to be kinder and more long-suffering with those who are in the darkness of the heart,' he ended, and left it at that.

If the Misses Carter had been present, it's doubtful they would have known the words were directed at the likes of them.

The Sugden family offered their condolences to Freda Gimbel, who accepted them with restraint. Davey and Martin, looking quite different even after a short absence, looked bewildered. Kathy kept in the background, a little behind her mother and her brothers. She said nothing to anyone.

Soon it was known that Mrs Gimbel had gone back to her job in Gloucestershire, with Davey. Martin's compassionate leave was over – he had gone back to camp.

'I can't bear to think of it,' Annie murmured to her father as they sat over late-night cocoa in the kitchen. 'Up there all by herself ...'

Sam sighed. 'She's the best of the Gimbels,' he remarked. 'Never had much time for them, and I'm not going to say I had, just because Jim Gimbel's dead. Freda Gimbel always struck me as self-centred ... But Kathy did her best in face of big problems. She's a good lass.'

Annie didn't say that her father's attitude had added to Kathy's problems, but it was in the mind of both. After a moment Sam said, 'What's Joe going to do? When she has to leave Holly Farm, I mean?'

'I don't know. I don't think he knows himself.'

'He expecting her to go back to Demdyke?'

His daughter got up and began to side the cocoa cups. 'If he is,' she said in a low voice, 'he's in for a disappointment, I think.'

Matt came in a moment later, from a date with Lucy Stubbs. For a time it had seemed as if Lucy had lost interest in Matt, after the mix-up over an evening date. But when Dolly Acaster walked out on the village concert it was Lucy who rallied round, finished the scene-painting, and saved the show. Annie was divided between pleasure and alarm – she didn't altogether like Lucy, who had a very bossy streak in her. But she was glad

Matt hadn't been too downcast when Dolly disappeared from the scene.

'Fine night,' Matt said, hanging up his jacket. 'Walked home – stars were a treat.'

'Aye, I saw them when I went to say goodnight to Bess,' Sam agreed.

Annie got Matt's cocoa for him. He drank a mouthful or two, lost in thoughts of his evening perhaps. Then he said suddenly, 'Hey! Know what I saw? Lowthwaite's taxi going down t'lane from Holly Farm.'

'The taxi?'

'Aye. Couldn't see who were in it, of course – it's dark. But I reckon that were Kathy.'

'She's never going?' Sam cried. 'What about stock?'

'Oh, they were saying in t'Woolpack that Tim Polwood's to go in night and morning till t'new tenant comes in.'

'She can't have gone,' Annie said. 'Wi'out a word?'

'Ring up and see, Annie,'

'Nay –'

'Ring up! What we got that confounded contraption for?' insisted Sam, who hated the telephone.

Annie fell in with his wish and dialled the number of Holly Farm, but though the bell rang and rang, no one replied.

'D'you think Joe knows?' Matt said.

They all stared at each other. No one knew how things stood between Joe and Kathy. And Annie pictured Joe in Demdyke, alone in the little house he had bought for her. Alone again ... it seemed unfair.

When Joe arrived next morning to start the day, no one mentioned Kathy. Matt worked alongside him until they went in for breakfast, and still it hadn't become clear to him whether Joe knew she was gone.

The meal was oddly strained. Joe looked from one to the other, but asked no questions. As they got up to go about their separate chores, Matt took Annie to one side. 'Should I say anything?'

'I'll do it, Matt.'

He was relieved. He was too fond of Joe to want to give him this blow. He went out quickly in Joe's tracks, for they were to take feed to the four-acre. When Annie came out at mid-morning with their coffee, he saw her lead Joe to a quiet spot by the dyke, where they spoke together in low tones.

It was easy to see from the sudden jerk of Joe's head that he had had a big surprise.

'Why didn't you tell me this morning?' he demanded.

'I thought she'd maybe send you some sort of message.'

'You say she left last night?'

'About ten. Matt saw her – at least he thinks it was her.'

'You should have told me at breakfast, Ma! All this time wasted . . .'

'What are you going to do, lad?'

'Go and find her,' he said.

Though she might wonder if it was a wise decision, she knew it was inevitable. He hurried to Matt.

'Where was the taxi headed when you saw it last night, Matt?'

'It were headed away from me – towards Hotten road.'

'Did you actually see Kathy?'

Matt shook his head. 'It were dark, Joe.'

Joe frowned. 'I'd best go up to t'farm just to make sure she really went last night. You can manage on your own for a bit, eh?'

'Aye, I can get on with unloading.'

Joe hurried away, leaving his mother and Matt gazing after him. 'He'll not find her at Holly Farm,' Matt murmured.

'You see, Matt,' Annie added, 'I don't think she wants him to find her.'

Matt hesitated. 'I don't really see why she . . . I mean, why dunt she have a word – let him know what's on?'

'She's running away, Matt.'

'Well, in a way – from Beckindale –'

'From Joe.'

'But Joe's done nowt.'

'She knows that.'

'Then why's she blaming him?'

'She's blaming herself – for wanting him.'

Joe spent all morning trying to get on Kathy's tracks. He found the farmhouse locked and empty. The livestock had been cared for, the cows milked, the poultry fed and watered – Tim Polwood had clearly been here earlier. Yet the place lacked those signs of occupation – nothing left about for immediate use, no washing blowing on the line.

He drove into Beckindale to speak to Andy Lowthwaite, who ran the hire car service as a one-man business. From him he could find out where Kathy had been taken. But Andy had taken a retired couple to Knaresborough for the day.

'He won't be back until teatime,' Mrs Lowthwaite said. 'Can I take a message?'

'Nay,' Joe said. 'Thanks, Mrs Lowthwaite.' How did you leave a message asking the whereabouts of the person who was supposed to be closest in the world to you?

Mr Hockley didn't know where she had gone – didn't even know she had gone, and looked perturbed at the news. 'I felt ... last time I saw her ... she really wasn't in a fit state to be making decisions about her future.'

'Did she mention about plans?'

'Her mother said she could come to the place in Gloucestershire where she's working now – Pelling Place, its called. I've got the telephone number if you'd like it.'

'Thanks, vicar.'

But Mrs Gimbel didn't know where Kathy had gone. She almost sounded vexed that Joe should ask her. 'Always a law unto herself, our Kathy,' she said. 'I invited her here – she as good as told me she'd rather die than live with me again.'

The words were used casually, but they haunted Joe after he'd put the phone down. 'Rather die ...' But Kathy was a sensible lass. She wasn't like her father, hunted by convictions that made life unbearable.

But then he thought of her words: 'If you had my conscience ...'

Everybody felt guilt to some degree. There wasn't a single

soul who thought he'd done everything perfectly, treated his fellow man with utter justice, fulfilled all his obligations. Joe himself knew what it was to feel guilt. He had been resentful of his dead father, less than fair to his elder brother, impatient with Henry ... Somewhere in a book at school he'd read something about 'I could accuse me of such things that it were better my mother had not borne me' – somebody in Shakespeare had said that. Even at school, Joe had known exactly what it meant, and he knew now that Kathy was bowed under a burden of guilt that might crush her.

It was just possible that even Kathy might surrender to feelings like that, and do something silly.

He went to Hotten in search of her. She had friends there, at the coffee bar. But Mrs Small hadn't seen her. 'I were that sorry to hear about her Dad ... I do wish she'd come and have a chat. Poor love, I'd do all I could for her if she needed a shoulder to cry on ... I know what it is to suffer,' said Mrs Small, looking dramatic and thinking about her latest love affair.

And Joe thought, 'No, Kathy wouldn't come here. Betty Small is all right when you're a bit down, but when you're really suffering, she'd be unbearable.'

So where? He turned and drove to Littlewell: they used to go there to a shop that sold paint and paper, when they were redecorating at Demdyke. Kathy had said Littlewell was a nice little place. But he didn't find her there, nor at Loudwick which was quiet and flat on a non-market day.

Connelton. She'd been at Connelton one day when she went out. He went there, looked for her in the Feathers and among the shops that sold souvenirs and antiques.

He had to get back for milking. Or at least, it was as well to go home and take a moment to think. Matt and his grandfather could have done the milking without him but happen the familiar routine would make his thought processes more clear.

It was while he was washing down that he remembered Bim. Bim – what was it – Boothroyd? Kathy had had some sort of relationship with him, she'd explained that he'd been a friend of Martin's. But Bim was on the road, doing one-night stands with his group. How the devil did you get in touch with a chap like that?

He went to the Woolpack as soon as he had cleaned up, to ask Amos how to get in touch with an entertainer who was touring. Amos was a reporter (or so he said) for the *Hotten Courier*. He ought to know things like that.

'I . . . er . . . I think the editor of the show page would know that,' Amos mumbled. He had really no idea whether that was true, but it sounded likely.

'D'you know him? Could you ring and find out for me?'

'Oh, 'course I know him,' Amos lied. 'What's this feller you want to track down?'

With the name written painstakingly on a slip of paper, Amos went to the phone. When he was connected he asked for the news editor, who was the man he usually contacted. 'E-er . . . Mr McDonald . . . could you put me through to the show page editor?' he faltered.

'Show page editor?' barked McDonald. 'What d'you think this is – the *Sunday Express*? I do the entertainments column.'

'Oh – ah – er . . .' said Amos, as if he were being put through to someone else. 'I'm trying to find out the whereabouts of a folksinger called Bim Boothroyd. A local chap – I thought you might keep track of him.'

'Boothroyd . . . Boothroyd . . . let's see . . . aye, he's on tour in Yorkshire at the moment.'

'Is that so? Could you tell me where he's playing tonight? Someone's interested in going there.'

'You amaze me,' McDonald said with a laugh. 'I didn't know he had any fans as keen as that. Well, he's in Northallerton tonight, at the Cloth Mill Club, according to my information.'

Joe was grateful and rather impressed when Amos turned back with the address. He went to the public phone and got the number from directory enquiries. But when he was put through he was told Bim Boothroyd wasn't at the club. 'Not due for more than an hour,' said the manager. 'His first performance is at seven-thirty. No reason for him to turn up much before that.'

'Can you tell me where he is now?'

'How should I know?' said the manager, irritated. 'Probably driving here from his last gig.'

There was nothing for it but to go to Northallerton. When he thought about it, he felt it was better than trying to speak to him on the phone. Bim might not want to tell him anyhing, even supposing he had informatiou.

The drive to Northallerton was easy once he got on to the motorway, but it was forty-six miles and he had had a long day already. When he got there he had still to find the Cloth Mill Club, but luckily a teenage girl in a long skirt and wooden beads was going there and accepted a lift to show him the way.

'Admission one pound, temporary membership one pound,' said the doorman.

'I don't want to come in,' Joe said. 'I just want to speak to Bim Boothroyd.'

'He's just about to go on stage,' the doorman said importantly. 'Can't disturb the artiste. You going to wait out here? It'll be about an hour.'

'No, I'll come in.'

'Admission one pound, temporary membership one pound.'

Joe had to admit that Bim and his group were rather good. They played well and without too much gimmickry. They gave good value for money and went on for more than an hour, so that it was nearly eleven before they finally stepped off the little dais that served as platform. At once they were surrounded by wellwishers offering to buy them a drink before the licencing hours ended.

Joe worked his way through to tap Bim on the shoulder. 'Can I speak to you?'

'Just a minute, eh? I'd like to sit down with my friends –'

'It's important. My name's Joe Sugden.'

Bim turned. 'Oh,' he said. 'Come on, then – we can go out into the passage.' He led the way.

'I'm looking for Kathy,' Joe began without preamble. 'Do you know where she is?'

'No,' Bim said. 'Don't you?'

'I wouldn't be asking if I knew.'

'Huh!' It was a grunt of dislike. 'So she walked out on you, did she? Serves you right. From what I gathered, you were giving her a hell of a time.'

Joe coloured, but held on to his temper. 'Listen, I didn't come to hear your opinion – I want to know where Kathy is.'

'I've no idea.' Then Bim seemed to realise what Joe was saying. 'Are you telling me she's just vanished?'

Joe nodded. 'The farm's been sold up. She could have stayed on till the new tenant –'

'Farm?' said Bim. 'But she lived in a little place in Beckindale. I dropped her off there –'

'Her father's farm. She went back there.'

'What on earth for? He was a right old tyrant, Martin always said.'

'He died.'

'What?'

'It was in the papers. You didn't see it?'

'I only ever read the show page,' Bim said with a rueful half-smile. 'Sorry, I seem to have got on the wrong foot with you. What's happened, exactly?'

In a few words Joe filled him in. Bim shook his head. 'A bad scene, brother. You don't think she's . . . you know . . . done something rash?'

'I keep telling myself she's not the sort. You really don't know where she is?'

'Nope.'

'Did she ever mention any place she thought of going? Any plans? Hopes?'

'Listen, man,' Bim said gently, smoothing back his shaggy hair, 'the only hopes Kathy had depended on *you*.'

It was early morning when Joe got back to Beckindale. He snatched a couple of hours' sleep before pulling himself out of bed for milking. As soon as he walked into the mistle Matt said, 'Any luck?'

'Not a sign.'

'She's all right, Joe. Don't worry about it.'

Joe looked at him. 'What's the use of saying that, Matt?'

Later in the morning Matt took the calves to Hotten market. He was taking Lucy Stubbs with him, since it was her day off from the Advisory Service and he had promised her lunch in the Lamb.

Joe had an appointment with Henry in the back room of the Woolpack, to go through invoices for the half-yearly audit. Henry said gruffly, 'Listen, lad, I wouldn't push my nose in, but if there's owt I can do ...?'

'Nothing anybody can do, really,' Joe said. 'Thanks all the same.'

'You don't look too good, you know.'

'A bit short on sleep, that's all.'

They worked over the papers, hardly hearing the phone when it rang. Amos came through to summon Joe. 'It's Matt – ringing from a phone box so be quick.'

Joe hurried to take the receiver. He thought something had gone wrong with the calves for sale.

'Listen, Joe, I've seen Kathy!'

'Where? In Hotten?'

'She's actually in the market building. Lucy spotted her first.'

'You're sure it's her?'

'We both saw her. I'm sure.'

'She all right?' Joe asked, holding his breath.

'Looks all right. What do you want us to do, Joe?'

'Nowt. I'm coming.'

He hurried back to Henry. 'We'll have to finish this another time, Henry. Matt's seen Kathy in Hotten.'

'Right you are, lad,' Henry said.

'Let Ma know, will you? She's worried sick though she doesn't say owt.'

'I'll see to it.'

The drive to Hotten was so familiar that Joe scarcely noticed it. He found Matt and Lucy waiting for him inside the main entrance to the market block. The day's business was over, the dealers had gone to lunch and the stock had been loaded into trucks to go to their new owners. The place echoed to their voices as the three of them went in.

'We called her,' Matt said. 'She either didn't hear or didn't reply.'

'It was noisy, of course,' Lucy put in.

'You know what it's like here when bidding's going on,' Matt agreed.

'Was she buying or selling or what?'

'Just walking across. We didn't go after her because we were in the crowd where our calves were coming up.' Matt hesitated. 'We did all right with 'em – eights.'

'That'll please Henry,' Joe said. He moved away. 'I'll just take a look round.'

'Aye,' Matt said. 'Lucy and me'll be in the Lamb if you want us ...'

But Joe was gone already.

When he saw Kathy at last it took him by surprise although he was searching for her. She was carrying a sheaf of papers and had that air of going somewhere for a purpose. He called. His voice echoed in the empty building. She wheeled.

She said nothing as he hastened along the stone-floored corridor to reach her.

'Where have you been?' he demanded when they were face to face. 'I've been out all night looking for you.'

'Have you? There was no need for that.'

'But where have you been? You didn't leave any word –!'

'I've been in Hotten.'

'But I asked for you at the coffee bar –'

'I've not been to see Betty. I've been busy. I had to move into my new flat.'

'New flat?'

'My employer fixed me up with it.'

'Kathy, what are you talking about? What employer? I thought you might like to come and work at Emmerdale – not be cooped up at Demdyke –'

'I've got a job, Joe,' she said, moving her arms so that the sheaf of papers fluttered in the cool draught of the market hall. 'I'm working for Fletcher and Arkwright – stock clerk for the market.'

'But . . . since when?'

'I came to enquire ages ago.' She bit her lip. 'It was the day my Dad died.'

'You mean – you've known ever since then that you were coming here?'

'I didn't *know* . . . I applied for the job, didn't know I'd get it. But they rang me Friday.'

'Kathy!'

'It's a good job. I think I'll enjoy it.'

He gathered himself together. 'Well, all right – you stick with it if you want to. You can drive in from Demdyke every day –'

'No.'

'I don't see why not. When we're wed you can give up this flat –'

'No, Joe. Don't go on.'

'But that was our plan, Kath. And the divorces –'

'I'll never marry you, Joe. I couldn't. Not after what's happened.'

'We just had some hard words, love. Everybody does that –'

'I mean about my father.' Her face seemed suddenly to collapse then put itself together again. 'I killed him, Joe. No, don't tell me I'm talking rubbish because I know I'm not. Dad wasn't all he might have been as a father, happen, but he believed in things – serious things. And us – living together like that in the village – openly . . .' Her voice trailed off for a moment. Then she said, 'He couldn't bear it. That's what killed him. And I was so stubborn I wouldn't see what it was doing to him.'

'You're wrong, Kathy –'

'Nay, I was stubborn and selfish! I hated it when folk gossiped about us – what must it have been like for Dad? Who *believed* it was wrong?'

Joe stared at her, his dark eyes as full of pain as her own.

'Look, love, you can't live your life how others think it should be.'

'You can try. You can try at least to put yourself in their place. And I never did, Joe. And we know what it did to him, don't we.'

'He did most of it to himself, Kathy. He tormented himself –'

'He wouldn't have had so much to torment himself with, if it hadn't been for me.'

Joe fetched a deep sigh. 'You're not going to hear a word against him, are you?'

'No, Joe, I'm not.'

'So where does that leave us?'

'It's over.'

'Just like that?'

She nodded.

For a long, long moment they stood looking at each other. Then he turned on his heel and left the market.

Matt and Lucy waited around for Joe but when he didn't show up they made their way home. Matt dropped Lucy off before heading for Emmerdale.

Annie was waiting for him with anxiety. 'Did you find Kathy? What happened, Matt?'

'Don't rightly know. I think he found her, Ma. He didn't come near us again, though we waited nigh on two hours.'

'He'll be back for his tea,' Sam put in. 'You can get the news from him then.'

Annie gazed out of the window at the lane leading away into the fold of the dales. 'He won't be in for tea,' she said.

'Did he say that? I don't remember him saying that.'

'He won't be in,' she said with conviction.

Later she went out to take some scraps to the geese. She stood for a long moment in the strong wind blowing from Blea Head, her apron flapping, her hair tugged back.

Something told her that Kathy was done with Beckindale. The things that had happened to her there could never be blotted out. If only, she thought, if only you could make young people see ... But what was the use of regretting their obstinate courage, their flamboyant bravado! They had done what they had done – and it had all gone wrong.

What was that old proverb? 'Take what you want, says God – and pay for it.'

Kathy was paying for it. A higher price than Joe, because Kathy felt the blame lay on her shoulders.

And also because Kathy had no one to turn to. For Joe, at least, there was always his family and the enduring firmness of the life at Emmerdale; but Kathy had only her weak, self-centred mother and a family that had broken up.

A fresh start ... Perhaps everything would go better for the girl if she made a fresh start ...

Annie straightened her shoulders. Every day was a fresh start, really. Tomorrow Joe would come back for the usual routine of milking, crop-spraying, fence-mending – the unending chores that make up the farmer's round. In those familiar tasks, perhaps he'd find the necessary impulse towards a fresh start without Kathy.

If he needed help, she would always be at hand.